MACMILLAN READERS
INTERMEDIATE LEVEL

THOMAS HARDY

Tess of the d'Urbervilles

Retold by John Escott

MACMILLAN

MACMILLAN READERS
INTERMEDIATE LEVEL

Founding Editor: John Milne

The Macmillan Readers provide a choice of enjoyable reading materials for learners of English. The series is published at six levels – Starter, Beginner, Elementary, Pre-intermediate, Intermediate and Upper.

Level control
Information, structure and vocabulary are controlled to suit the students' ability at each level.

The number of words at each level:

Starter	about 300 basic words
Beginner	about 600 basic words
Elementary	about 1100 basic words
Pre-intermediate	about 1400 basic words
Intermediate	about 1600 basic words
Upper	about 2200 basic words

Vocabulary
Some difficult words and phrases in this book are important for understanding the story. Some of these words are explained in the story and some are shown in the pictures. From Pre-intermediate level upwards, words are marked with a number like this: ...[3]. These words are explained in the Glossary at the end of the book.

Answer keys
Answer keys for the *Points for Understanding* and the *Exercises* sections can be found at www.macmillanenglish.com

Contents

A Note About the Author

Thomas Hardy was born in the small village of Higher Bockhampton on the 2nd of June 1840. The village is in the county[1] of Dorset, in the south of England.

Thomas's father was a builder and stonemason – he cut and shaped pieces of stone for building. Thomas's mother loved reading and she owned many books. She encouraged Thomas to read all kinds of books. Thomas was the eldest child. He had a brother and two sisters.

Thomas Hardy went to a good school in Dorchester, the nearest town to his home. He learnt Latin, French, German and Mathematics, as well as Literature, Science and Art.

When he was sixteen, Thomas left school and started to work for an architect. The architect drew designs of new buildings and planned ways to repair old ones.

In 1862, Thomas moved to London and got a job in the office of a famous architect. Hardy enjoyed the time that he was in London. He often visited theatres and art galleries, and he read lots of books. Soon he began to write poetry, although none of his poems were published at this time.

In 1867, Thomas decided to return to Dorchester. In the town, he worked as an architect's assistant. But now he knew that he wanted to be a writer. He wrote a novel, but no one wanted to publish it. This did not stop Thomas writing, and soon he was working on a second novel.

In 1870, the architect sent Thomas to the county of Cornwall, in the far west of England. Thomas had to look at the old church in the village of St Juliot. His job was to make drawings of the church. He also had to find out if the church could be repaired or rebuilt.

This visit to Cornwall changed Thomas's life completely because he fell in love with a lady named Emma Lavinia Gifford. Emma had fair hair and blue eyes and she liked poetry and novels. She also wanted to be a writer.

Emma encouraged Thomas to write more novels, and in 1871 one of these novels was published. It was called *Desperate Remedies*. Thomas did not earn much money from the book. However, his next novel, *Under the Greenwood Tree* (1872), was more successful. It is a story about working people in Dorset at the time of Thomas's own father and grandfather. The story is unusual because it ends happily. Many of Thomas Hardy's novels have sad endings.

In 1874, Thomas Hardy's first great novel – *Far From the Madding Crowd* – was published. It was very successful and Thomas and Emma got married. They went to live in Dorchester. They lived in a large house called Max Gate, which Hardy had designed himself. In the twenty years that followed, Thomas wrote more successful novels and short stories. His stories were set in an area of England which he called Wessex. Wessex included the counties of Devon, Berkshire, Dorset, Wiltshire, Somerset and Hampshire.

Hardy's best-known novels are: *The Return of the Native* (1878), *The Trumpet-Major* (1880), *The Mayor of Casterbridge* (1886), *The Woodlanders* (1887), *Tess of the d'Urbervilles* (1891) and *Jude the Obscure* (1896).

After 1895, when he finished *Jude the Obscure*, Thomas Hardy wrote no more novels. *Jude the Obscure* is a very unhappy story about death. It tells about people's loss of belief in religion. It tells about quarrels[2] between working people and well-educated people. And it tells about sexual relationships between people who are not married. Many readers were shocked by this book and suddenly Hardy was no longer a popular writer. For the last thirty years of his life, he wrote only poetry. Many books of his poems were published during this time.

The last years of Thomas and Emma's marriage were not happy. Thomas did not speak to Emma and he did not care when she was ill. But when she died in 1912, Thomas felt guilty[3] and unhappy. Suddenly he wrote many poems about Emma and about the early days of their relationship. In 1914, Hardy married again. His new wife, Florence Dugdale, was very much younger than Thomas. But Thomas could not forget his first wife. He made Florence very unhappy because he thought about Emma all the time, and he wrote many poems about her.

Thomas Hardy died on 11th January 1928. His body was buried in Westminster Abbey, the famous church in London. But Hardy's heart was buried with Emma, beside a church in Dorset.

A Note About This Story

Most of Thomas Hardy's stories are about the people who worked on the farms and in the small villages in the country[4] area which he called Wessex. In the 1880s, many country people were poor and their lives were hard. They did things in the same way that their parents and grandparents had done them. They also did special things on special days of the year – these were their customs. One of their customs was to celebrate[5] spring – the time when trees and plants begin to grow again, and young animals are born.

In the nineteenth century the country people of Wessex worked very hard every month of the year. They did not earn much money. Farm work was dirty and difficult. Every family member had to work – even small children. Until 1886, country children did not go to school. They helped their mothers and fathers. After 1886, all children were able to go to school for a few years so that they learnt to read, write and count. After working very hard, farm workers often went to inns and drank large amounts of beer. When they were drunk, they could forget about their troubles.

Most country people lived in cottages. These small, simple houses and the large farms where the people worked, belonged to rich landowners. Landowners paid farmers to live on their land and look after their farms. Each year, the farmers of Wessex hired[6] many farm workers to work on the farms. If there was no work, families had to leave their homes and find somewhere else to live.

At this time, most country people walked, or travelled in vehicles pulled by horses. Railway lines had not yet been built to all parts of the country.

Farm workers did many different jobs. In the spring, they planted the cereal crops[7] or vegetable crops in the fields. They looked after the farm buildings. They made and repaired the hedges[8] and walls which surrounded the fields. Farm workers also looked after the animals. Shepherds looked after herds of sheep. Dairy farmers kept cows and sold their milk. The dairy farmers hired men and women to look after the herds of cows. These workers were called dairymen and dairymaids.

By the 1880s, machines were coming onto the farms to help the farm workers. But these machines were noisy and dangerous. Workers had to work faster and for more hours so that they could keep the machines running well. When the crops had finished growing, they were harvested[9]. The grain from the cereal crops was taken to mills[10] where it was made into flour for bread.

Many families in country villages grew vegetables and fruit on allotments[11]. They also kept a few chickens and sometimes they kept a pig. On one day in each week, there was a market in the larger villages or towns. Families could take the food that they did not need for themselves to these markets and sell it.

The People in This Story

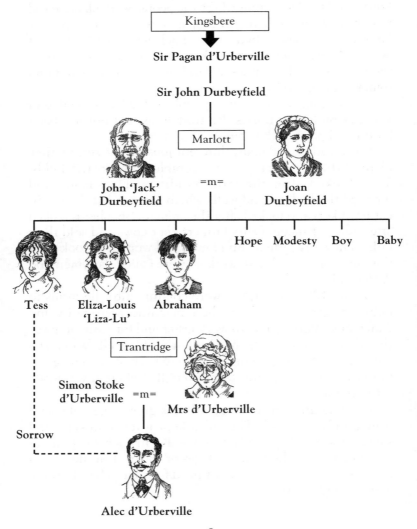

Kingsbere

Sir Pagan d'Urberville

Sir John Durbeyfield

Marlott

John 'Jack' Durbeyfield =m= Joan Durbeyfield

Hope Modesty Boy Baby

Tess Eliza-Louis 'Liza-Lu' Abraham

Trantridge

Simon Stoke d'Urberville =m= Mrs d'Urberville

Sorrow

Alec d'Urberville

| Parson Tringham | Fred | Farmer Groby | Mercy Chant | Mrs Brooks |

Emminster

Reverend James Clare =m= Mrs Clare

Felix   Cuthbert   Angel

Talbothays

| Head Dairyman Richard Crick | Mrs Crick | Retty Priddle | Izz Huett | Marian | Jonathan Kail |

9

The Places in This Story

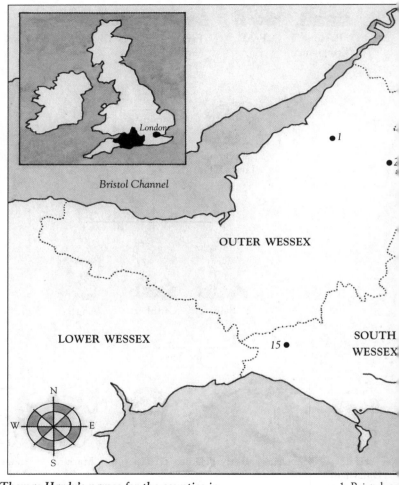

London

Bristol Channel

OUTER WESSEX

LOWER WESSEX

SOUTH
WESSEX

●1

●2

15 ●

N
W — E
S

Thomas Hardy's names for the counties in
southwest England:

Lower Wessex = Devon   Mid-Wessex = Wiltshire

North Wessex = Berkshire   Outer Wessex = Somerset

South Wessex = Dorset   Upper Wessex = Hampshire

1 Bristol
2 Bath
3 Melchest
4 Shaston
5 Marlott

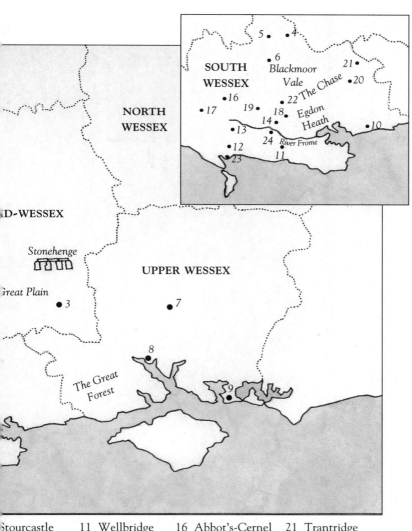

Stourcastle	11	Wellbridge	16	Abbot's-Cernel	21	Trantridge
Wintoncester	12	Overcombe	17	Chalk-Newton	22	Bulbarrow
Southampton	13	Casterbridge	18	Kingsbere	23	Budmouth
Portsmouth	14	Weatherbury	19	Flintcomb-Ash	24	Talbothays Farm
Sandbourne	15	Emminster	20	The Chase		

1

Tess

One evening in May, a middle-aged man was walking from the village of Shaston to his home in the village of Marlott. He was carrying an empty basket in one hand.

Early that same day, the man had been to the market in Shaston to sell the eggs from his chickens. When he had sold all the eggs, he had gone to an inn[12]. He had stayed there all day, drinking beer. Now the man was very drunk, and he could not walk in a straight line.

After some time he met an elderly parson[13] riding a grey horse.

'Good night, Parson Tringham,' said the man with the basket.

'Good night, Sir John[14],' said the parson, as he rode past the drunken man.

The man stopped and turned round.

'Excuse me, sir,' he said. 'We met on this road at this time last week. I said "goodnight", and you replied "Goodnight, Sir John" to me then, too.'

'Perhaps I did,' said the parson.

'Why do you call me "Sir John"?' asked the man. 'My name is Jack Durbeyfield.'

The parson rode on a little further, then he stopped his horse and turned back.

'As you know, Durbeyfield,' said the parson, 'the name "Jack" is often used instead of John. And a little time ago, I discovered something interesting about the history of your family. Durbeyfield, you are a descendant[15] of the very old and noble[16] family called d'Urberville. Sir Pagan d'Urberville, who lived hundreds of years ago in this county of Dorset, was a famous knight.'

13

'I've never heard that before,' said Durbeyfield.

'It's true,' said the parson. 'Let me look at you, Durbeyfield. I've seen portraits[17] of members of the d'Urberville family. Yes, Durbeyfield. Your nose and chin look like the noses and chins of the people in those pictures. The d'Urberville family once had manor houses[18] all over this part of England. There have been many d'Urbervilles named Sir John. You could have been "Sir John" yourself.'

'Is that right, Parson Tringham?' said Durbeyfield. 'I am a d'Urberville? Well, I've heard that my family once had money and land. And maybe the Durbeyfields were once called d'Urberville. But we are poor now. My grandfather had secrets. He never talked about his family. But where do the d'Urbervilles live now, Parson Tringham?'

'There are no more members of the noble d'Urberville family,' answered the parson. 'They are all dead.'

'And where do their bodies lie?'

'At Kingsbere,' said the parson. 'In the churchyard[19] there.'

'What about our family's land and houses?'

'You don't have any.'

'Oh. Will we ever be a noble family again?' asked Durbeyfield.

'Ah – I can't tell you that,' replied the parson. 'I don't know.'

'What can I do about it, sir?'

'Nothing,' said the parson. 'You can't do anything about it. It's an interesting piece of history, that's all.'

'Well, Parson Tringham, will you come and have a drink of beer with me at the Pure Drop Inn?'

'No, thank you, Durbeyfield,' said the parson. 'You've had enough beer already.' And he rode on.

Jack Durbeyfield sat down at the side of the road with his basket. After a few minutes, a young man walked past.

'Fred!' shouted Durbeyfield. 'Carry this basket for me.'

The young man turned to look at him. 'Jack Durbeyfield, you can't shout at me and give me orders!' he said. 'You're not a rich gentleman.'

'Ah, but I've just heard that I'm a member of a noble family,' Durbeyfield said. 'Jack Durbeyfield is not my real name. My true name is Sir John d'Urberville!'

'Oh?' said the young man.

'Take this basket and go to Marlott,' said Durbeyfield. 'Go to the Pure Drop Inn and tell the innkeeper to send me a horse and carriage[20]. After that, go on to my house with the basket. Tell my wife to stop her work and wait until I come home. I've got good news.' He gave the young man some money. 'This is for you.'

'Oh, well, yes, *Sir John*,' said Fred, smiling. He was happy to play Durbeyfield's game now that money was in his hand.

Just then, they heard the sound of music coming from the village.

'What's that?' said Durbeyfield.

'It's the May Walk and Dance[21], Sir John. Your daughter will be there.'

'Of course. I forgot about that. Well, run to Marlott and ask the innkeeper to send that carriage. Perhaps I'll drive to see the dancing.'

———

The village of Marlott lies between the hills of the beautiful Vale of Blackmoor[22] in the county of Dorset. Blackmoor Vale was once full of trees, but most of these are gone now.

Each woman in the May Dance was wearing a white dress and carrying flowers. This evening, they walked down the road and around the Pure Drop Inn. They were about to go into one of the fields beside the inn, when suddenly one of the women pointed towards the road.

'Look, Tess Durbeyfield,' she said. 'There's your father, riding home in a carriage!'

One of the young women turned her head quickly. Tess Durbeyfield was a very pretty girl, with large, grey-blue eyes and soft, pale skin. She was the only dancer who was wearing a red ribbon²³ in her dark hair.

Jack Durbeyfield was travelling along the road in a carriage which belonged to the landlord of the Pure Drop Inn. The driver was a large woman who was a servant at the inn. Durbeyfield was singing about knights and noble families, and waving his hands above his head.

The dancers began to laugh. Tess Durbeyfield was very embarrassed and her face blushed red.

'My father is riding in the carriage because his own horse is resting today,' she said quickly.

But the other women laughed again and said, 'He's drunk!'

'I won't walk with you if you laugh at him!' Tess said to the women. And her eyes began to fill with tears.

The dancers said nothing more. They opened the gate at the entrance of the field and in a few minutes, the dancing began.

At first, only girls danced together. Later, after their work was finished, the men from the village would arrive to dance with them.

Among the people who were watching the girls, there were three brothers. The young gentlemen were students and they were on a walking holiday in Wessex. Their names were Angel Clare, Felix Clare and Cuthbert Clare. They stopped at the field to ask about the dancing. The two older brothers wanted to continue along the road, but the youngest was in no hurry²⁴ to leave the field. He went through the gate.

'What are you going to do, Angel?' asked the oldest brother.

'I think that I'll dance,' said the youngest brother. 'Why don't we all stop here for a minute or two?'

16

'My father is riding in the carriage because his own horse
is resting today,' Tess said quickly.

'No, no!' said Felix Clare. 'We don't want to dance with these common[25] country girls. One of our friends or relations might see us! Come with us now, or it will be dark before we get to Stourcastle.'

'I'll follow you in five minutes, Felix,' said the younger man.

So the two older brothers went on along the road and the youngest brother walked across the field. He went towards the nearest group of girls.

'Where are your dancing-partners[26]?' he asked.

'They've not finished their work yet,' said one of the girls. 'Will you be a dancing-partner, sir?'

'Yes!' said the young man. He looked at each of the girls, then he held the hand of the nearest dancer. This was not the girl who had spoken to him, and it was not Tess Durbeyfield.

Soon, the young men from the village arrived and all the girls had dancing-partners.

When the bell in the church clock rang six times, the young student said, 'I must leave!'

As he moved away from the dancers, Angel saw a girl standing by the hedge at the edge of the field. She had a red ribbon in her hair and she was looking at him. She seemed annoyed[27] because he had not chosen her as his dancing-partner. Suddenly Angel was sorry that he had not noticed[28] her earlier and asked her name.

Angel went away down the road and Tess left the dancers. She was worried about her father. She hurried home to her parents' cottage in the village. Her mother was waiting with the other children.

'Tess, I'm glad that you've come home,' Joan Durbeyfield said. 'I want to go and fetch your father from the inn. But first, I want to tell you what has happened.

'Your father has just heard some good news,' Tess's mother said. 'The Durbeyfields are members of the oldest and most noble family in the whole county! Our real name is d'Urberville!'

'Will it be good for us to be members of the d'Urberville family, mother?'

'Oh, yes!'

'But where *is* father?'

'Now don't be angry, Tess! Your poor father felt very weak[29] after he heard the news. So he went to Rolliver's Inn half an hour ago. He wants to get strong for his journey to Casterbridge market tomorrow.'

'He won't get strong drinking beer at an inn!' said Tess angrily. 'I'll go and get him.'

'No, Tess. I waited for you to come home. You must look after the children while *I* go and get him.'

Sixteen-year-old Tess was Mrs Durbeyfield's oldest child. There were six other children in the Durbeyfield family. Eliza-Louisa, called 'Liza-Lu', was twelve years old. Abraham was nine. Then came two more girls – Hope, aged eight, and Modesty, aged six. Then there was a three-year-old boy. The youngest child was a one-year-old baby.

Joan Durbeyfield was always happy to go and find her husband at Rolliver's Inn. She could sit with him for an hour or two and not worry about the children. It was eleven o'clock before all the family were in their beds.

———

At half-past one in the morning, Mrs Durbeyfield came into the large bedroom where Tess and her brothers and sisters slept. Tess opened her eyes immediately when the bedroom door opened.

'Your poor father can't go to Casterbridge market today,' Mrs Durbeyfield told her.

'Then I must go,' Tess said. 'Abraham can come with me.'

Tess and her younger brother got dressed. Then they went out to get their wagon and Prince, their old horse.

Minutes later, they began their journey. It was dark and Tess put a lantern[30] on the wagon. The brother and sister rode in the wagon without speaking until they passed the little town of Stourcastle.

'Tess,' said Abraham. 'Are you glad that we're a noble family?'

'No, I'm not specially glad[31],' she answered.

'But perhaps our noble relations will help you to marry a rich gentleman,' said Abraham.

'We have no noble relations!' said Tess. 'Who put that idea into your head[32]?'

'I heard mother and father talking about it,' said Abraham. 'There's a member of our family at Trantridge. She's a rich lady. Mother said that the lady will help you to marry a gentleman.'

Tess thought about this. Her brother went on talking, but she did not listen. After a few minutes, Abraham fell asleep. Tess sat back in the driving seat of the wagon. The sound of the horse's feet on the road made her feel tired. Soon, she fell asleep too.

Tess woke suddenly. Something had hit the wagon very hard. The wagon had stopped moving. She heard a terrible sound come from the horse, Prince.

Then she heard a shout. A man's voice said, 'Hey, there!'

The lantern on Tess's wagon had gone out, but another light was shining in her face. She jumped down on to the road.

The mail cart[33], which had been speeding[34] along the road, had driven into Tess's slow, unlighted wagon. Prince was badly hurt. Blood was pouring from a large wound in his chest. Suddenly he fell down onto the ground.

'You were driving on the wrong side of the road!' the mail cart man said to Tess. 'And your lantern was not lit. I didn't see you in the dark. I must go on with the mailbags. I'll send

Prince was badly hurt. Blood was pouring from a large wound in his chest.

somebody to help you as soon as I can. It will be daylight soon, so don't be afraid.' Then he got back onto his cart and drove away.

Tess stood and waited. Prince lay still on the road. His eyes were half-open and there was blood on the ground all around him. Their horse was dead.

'It was my fault[35]!' cried Tess, as tears fell from her eyes. 'What will father and mother do now? Abraham! Abraham!' She shook the sleeping child. 'Wake up! There has been an accident! Prince is dead, and it's my fault!'

———

'We must take the good luck with the bad luck, Tess,' Mrs Durbeyfield said that evening. 'It's bad luck that Prince was killed. But it's good luck that we discovered that we are a noble family at this time. A very rich lady – Mrs d'Urberville – lives on the edge of the hill called The Chase. You must go and tell her about us. You must tell her that we – the Durbeyfields – are her relations. You must ask her for some help.'

'Well, I killed Prince,' said Tess, sadly. 'It was my fault that our horse died in the accident. I must do something to help our family now. But don't expect Mrs d'Urberville to find me a rich husband!'

2

Alec d'Urberville

Early the next day, Tess walked to Shaston, and from there a van took her to Trantridge.

At the village of Trantridge, Tess got out of the van and walked up a hill. After a few minutes, she saw The Slopes – a large, new manor house which was surrounded by some land,

gardens and a little farm. Behind the house was The Chase –
a hill covered with trees.

'I thought that we were an old family, but this house and
farm are all new,' Tess said to herself. Suddenly, she wanted to
go home again.

The d'Urbervilles – or the Stoke-d'Urbervilles, as they
first called themselves – were not really d'Urbervilles at all.
The Stokes were from the north of England. The family had
given themselves the name of d'Urberville when they came
to live in the south of England. Of course, Tess did not know
this. Parson Tringham was right. John Durbeyfield and his
family were the only real d'Urbervilles in Wessex.

A tall young gentleman came out of the house. He was
about twenty-four years old, with dark brown eyes and a
black moustache.

'Well, my beauty[36],' he said, looking at Tess and smiling.
'What can I do for you? I'm Mr Alec d'Urberville. Have you
come to speak to me, or my mother?'

'Your mother, sir,' answered Tess.

'I'm afraid that you cannot speak to her. She is ill. What
do you want to talk to her about?'

'It – it's something foolish. I'm afraid to tell you,' Tess
replied.

'Tell me,' said the young man. 'I like foolish things.'

'I – I am from the same family as you, sir.'

'Oh! Are you poor relatives? Are you a member of the
Stoke family?'

'No, the d'Urberville family, sir.'

'Ah, yes. I meant to say the d'Urbervilles.'

'We are called Durbeyfield, but our parson discovered
that we are d'Urbervilles,' said Tess. 'Mother said that we are
the oldest part of the family. She wanted me to tell you this.
And I have to tell you that our horse died in an accident.'

Alec d'Urberville looked at Tess until she blushed.

23

'Well, where do you live, my pretty girl?' he asked. 'What do you do?'

Tess told him about her home in Marlott and her family. She told him that she helped her father to look after his chickens. Finally she said, 'I will go back to Marlott on the van from Trantridge, sir.'

'It's some time before the van returns,' he said. 'Until then, let's walk in the gardens. Do you like strawberries, my pretty cousin?'

As they walked through the gardens, Alec d'Urberville picked the sweet, red fruit and put some into a basket. Suddenly, he held one of the strawberries up to Tess's mouth. She was embarrassed. She did not want to eat the fruit from the young gentleman's fingers. But he smiled and kept asking her to eat the strawberry. At last, Tess blushed and opened her mouth. Then Alec d'Urberville picked some red flowers and put these in the basket too.

'What is your name?'

'Tess Durbeyfield,' she replied.

'And your horse died?'

'I – I killed him!' she said. And as she told him about the accident, her eyes filled with tears.

'Perhaps my mother can find work for you here,' he said. 'But you will not use the name of d'Urberville. You'll keep your name of Durbeyfield. All right, Tess?'

The next day, a letter came to the Durbeyfields' cottage. It was from Mrs d'Urberville. Joan Durbeyfield was excited.

'The old lady wants you to go and look after her chickens, Tess!' she said.

'But I didn't see her,' said Tess. 'I met her son.'

'Well, he spoke to his mother. And now she wants you to go to their farm,' said Mrs Durbeyfield.

'I don't want to go. I want to stay here with you and father,' Tess said.

He held one of the strawberries up to Tess's mouth.

Tess remembered how Alec d'Urberville had smiled at her. She remembered how he had called her 'beauty', and fed her strawberries.

'Why don't you want to go?' asked Mrs Durbeyfield.

'I – I don't know,' said Tess.

———

Tess tried to find work in Marlott, but there were no jobs for her. A week later, she came home one evening and found that all her family was very excited.

'A gentleman came here!' one of the children said.

'Mrs d'Urberville's son came here himself,' Tess's mother explained. 'He came to ask if you will look after his mother's chickens. The d'Urbervilles want an answer, Tess. What are you going to do?'

'I don't know,' said Tess. 'I killed the old horse, so I must help you to buy another one. I – I don't like Mr d'Urberville. But – yes – I'll go and work for his mother.'

'Mr d'Urberville is a very handsome gentleman!' Joan Durbeyfield told her husband. 'He'll marry Tess and she'll be a fine lady!'

———

The day came for Tess to go to The Slopes at Trantridge. Her mother went with her to the edge of Marlott village, and they waited. Then a van arrived to take Tess's luggage. A few minutes later, Alec d'Urberville arrived in a gig and Tess climbed into it. She said goodbye to her mother, and Alec d'Urberville drove away down the hill.

They were travelling at a very fast speed and Tess was frightened. But she tried not to show that she was afraid. She put her hand on d'Urberville's arm.

'Don't touch my arm,' he said. 'Put your arms around my waist.'

Tess held Alec's waist until the gig reached the bottom of the hill, then she took her hands away.

At the top of the next hill, Alec said, 'Put your arms around my waist again, my beauty!'

'No!' said Tess. And she held on to the seat of the gig as tightly as she could. She did not want to touch him.

Alec d'Urberville turned his head towards her and smiled. He stopped the horse.

'Let me kiss you, Tess, and I'll drive slowly,' he said.

'Will nothing else stop you from driving so fast?' she said.

But when Alec d'Urberville tried to kiss her, Tess moved her head away quickly.

'Now I'll kill both of us!' he said angrily.

He was going to make the horse leap forward again when Tess spoke.

'Oh, all right. You may kiss me, sir,' she said. 'But I thought that you would be kind to me. I don't want to kiss anybody.'

This time, Tess sat still and Alec kissed her. Immediately, she wiped her cheek with her handkerchief.

'You'll be sorry that you did that!' he told her. 'Let me kiss you again. And this time, no handkerchief!'

At that moment, Tess's hat blew off into the road and she jumped down to get it. 'I shall walk now,' she said.

'It's five or six miles to Trantridge,' said Alec.

'I don't care,' Tess replied.

Alec d'Urberville called her every bad name that he could think of.

'I hate you!' she told him. 'I'll go back to my mother!'

Suddenly, d'Urberville began to laugh. 'Listen,' he said. 'I'll never do that again, I promise.'

But she would not get into the gig again and ride with him. She walked beside the horse until they reached The Slopes manor house.

––––

Mrs d'Urberville's chickens lived inside an old cottage. The cottage stood in a garden surrounded by a wall. The wall was about four feet high and it had a wooden gate in it.

On the first morning after Tess arrived, a servant came from the manor house. She told Tess to take some of the chickens to the old lady. She also told her that Mrs d'Urberville was blind[37].

Mrs d'Urberville heard Tess and the servant come into the sitting-room of her big house. The old woman was sitting in a large chair. She had white hair and was about sixty years old. She was a widow. Her husband, Simon Stoke-d'Urberville, had died a year before.

'Are you the young woman who is looking after my birds?' Mrs d'Urberville asked. 'I hope that you will be kind to them.'

The blind old woman took the two chickens from Tess's arms and touched each bird carefully with her fingers. She checked that they were healthy[38] and gave them back to Tess.

Then she took the chickens from the servant and did the same thing.

'Can you whistle[39]?' she asked Tess. 'I want you to whistle to my birds every day. You must practise.'

'Yes, ma'am[40],' said Tess.

Mrs d'Urberville knew nothing about Tess's family. Alec had not told her that Tess was a d'Urberville. Tess did not know that Alec d'Urberville had not told his mother this information. But the young girl was not surprised at the way that the old woman gave orders about her chickens. Mrs d'Urberville was a great lady who lived in a great house.

Soon Tess was back in the walled garden. She began to practise whistling to the chickens. But she was surprised to find that she could not do it. She could *not* whistle. Tess blew air through her lips again and again but no sound came out.

Suddenly, she saw someone jump over the wall. It was Alec d'Urberville.

'Let me show you how to whistle, my pretty cousin!' he said.

'No, thank you!' said Tess, moving towards the cottage.

'I won't touch you,' said Alec.

'Oh, all right,' she said.

Alec showed her the way to whistle and, after a lot of practice, Tess found that she could do it too. In the weeks that followed, she began to feel more comfortable when Alec came to see her, which he often did.

———

Every Saturday night, workers from the farms near The Slopes went to Chaseborough, a small town near Trantridge. They went to inns and drank beer until they were very drunk. On Sundays, the farm workers slept most of the day.

After a few weeks, Tess began to go to Chaseborough with the farm workers. One Saturday night in September, Tess was waiting for her friends outside one of the inns. It was late. The workers were still drinking inside the inn. But Tess was tired and she wanted to go to her bed.

Suddenly she saw a small red light in the darkness. It was the end of a burning cigar. The man who was smoking the cigar was walking towards her.

'My pretty cousin!' said Alec d'Urberville. 'What are you doing here at this time of night?'

'I'm waiting for my friends,' she answered.

'I only have my horse with me,' he said. 'But I can get a carriage. I'll take you back to The Slopes.'

'No, thank you, sir,' she said. 'I'll wait for my friends. We will walk together.'

'All right,' he said, and moved away.

At last, a group of her friends came out of the inn. They had been drinking beer all evening and they were very drunk.

None of them could walk in a straight line. Tess began to walk back to the farm with them. But after a few minutes, the women started shouting and fighting. Tess wanted to get away from them.

Suddenly, Alec d'Urberville rode along the road. He stopped and turned his horse.

'Tess, get up here behind me!' he said. 'We'll get away from these screaming cats!'

Tess thought for a few seconds, then she got up onto the back of the horse with Alec d'Urberville.

They went along the road for some time without speaking. Then suddenly, fog[41] appeared all around them. The fog hid the road in front of them and the land on both sides of them. Soon Alec and Tess could see only a few feet in front of the horse.

'Tess,' Alec d'Urberville said after a few minutes. 'You don't like it when I kiss you. Why is that?'

'Because I don't love you,' answered Tess.

'Are you sure?' he said.

'Yes,' she replied. 'And I'm often angry with you.'

'Are you angry because I try to make love to you[42]?' asked Alec.

'Sometimes,' she said, after a moment.

'Are you angry *every* time that I try to make love to you?' he asked.

She did not answer, and they travelled on for a mile or two without speaking.

Tess was tired, and she could not see clearly in the fog. So she did not notice when they passed the road to Trantridge. They were now in a wood of tall, old trees. The fog made the great trees look like huge grey ghosts.

Alec turned and put his arm around Tess so that she did not fall off the horse.

'Where are we?' she asked in a tired voice.

'The Chase, my darling,' he replied. 'Tess, can't I be your lover?'

She moved on the horse's back. She was nervous and afraid.

'I – I don't know,' she said. 'I wish ... Oh, how can I say yes or no when I don't understand ... ?' She stopped speaking. She could not find the right words to finish her sentence.

Alec did not move his arm, and at first Tess did not try to push him away from her. But then she said, 'Let me get off the horse and walk back to the farm!'

'You can't walk to The Slopes, Tess,' said Alec. 'We're miles from Trantridge. And you'll get lost in the fog. *I* don't know exactly where we are. Listen to me. Wait here with the horse. I'll walk and find a road or a house. Then I'll come back for you.'

Before Tess could stop him, Alec kissed her and then they both got off the horse.

'Your father has a new horse now, and the children have some new toys,' Alec said.

'Did *you* buy the horse and the toys?' asked Tess. 'Oh, thank you.' But she did not feel happy. 'I – I almost wish that you hadn't.'

'Tess, don't you love me a little now?' Alec said.

'You have given help to my family and I'm grateful,' she said. 'But I don't – oh, I don't know!' She began to cry.

'Don't cry, dear girl,' said Alec, putting his coat on the ground. 'Sit down and wait for me. Are you cold?'

As he said this, he took a bottle from a pocket in the coat. He opened the bottle and held it to Tess's mouth.

'Drink this,' he said, 'it will warm you.' He pulled the coat around her body as she drank. 'Rest here,' he said. 'I'll come back soon.'

Tess heard Alec walk away, but she was suddenly very tired again and her eyes were closing.

When Alec returned, Tess was asleep. He looked down at her. She was so beautiful in her white dress.

'Tess!' he said softly.

She did not answer. There was darkness and silence all around them. Above them were the great trees of The Chase where the birds slept.

Alec d'Urberville lay down on the ground beside Tess. He moved closer and looked at her pale face. She was breathing softly and there were tears on her dark eyelashes.

After that night, Tess's life was never the same again.

3
The Child

It was early on a Sunday morning in October. Four months had passed since Tess had gone to work at Trantridge. Now she was walking up the hill towards Marlott. She was carrying a heavy basket in one hand and a bundle[43] containing the rest of her things in the other hand. At the top of the hill, Tess looked down on Blackmoor Vale and the village of Marlott.

The Vale always looked beautiful from the top of the hill. But it was even more beautiful today. Since she had last seen her home, Tess's life had changed. She was not the same innocent[44] girl who had left Marlott in June. She had learnt about wickedness[45]. She had learnt about the wicked way that rich men treated[46] weak, country girls.

Tess heard a noise and turned to look behind her. A horse and gig was coming up the hill and the driver was walking beside the tired horse. The man held up one of his hands and waved at Tess. She waited for him to reach her.

'Why did you leave The Slopes secretly, Tess?' Alec

Above them were the great trees of The Chase.

d'Urberville asked her. 'Nobody will stop you leaving, if that's what you want. I've been driving fast to catch you, just look at my poor horse.'

'I won't come back to your farm,' she said.

'That is what I thought,' Alec said. 'Well, get into the gig and I'll drive you home.'

Alec d'Urberville helped Tess up into the gig. She sat beside him without speaking. After a few minutes, they saw the village of Marlott.

Tess began to cry. Tears ran down her cheeks.

'Why are you crying?' d'Urberville asked in a cold voice.

'That village is my home. It's where I was born.'

'We are all born somewhere,' he replied.

'I wish that I'd *never* been born – there or anywhere else!' said Tess. 'I wish that I hadn't been born at all!'

'So why did you come to work in Trantridge? Not because you loved me. I know that.'

'That's true,' she said. 'If I loved you, I would not hate myself for my weakness. And I do hate myself. I hate what you did to me! I hate what we did. But I didn't understand what you were going to do until it was too late.'

'Every woman says that she doesn't understand until it's too late,' Alec said. 'But they don't mean the words that they say.'

'Some women *do* mean what they say!' Tess said, angrily.

He laughed. 'All right, I'm sorry. I'll pay you money. You will never have to work again. You can have clothes —'

'I'll never take anything from you!' she said. 'Never!'

'Well, my dear cousin,' Alec said. 'I suppose that I'm a bad person. I was born bad, I've lived bad and I'll probably die bad! But I won't be bad to you again, Tess. And if you're in trouble or if you need anything, write to me. I'm going to London for a time.'

Tess did not want Alec to take her into the village. She

got down from the gig and stood at the side of the road.

'Let me kiss you, my dear!' Alec said.

'If you want to,' she said, coldly.

Alec d'Urberville leant down and kissed her. Then he said, 'Cousin Tess, don't be sad. You're more beautiful than any woman in the county. And ... oh, will you come back with me? Please?'

'Never,' she replied.

'Then goodbye, cousin who I've known for four months,' he said. Then he turned the horse and drove off.

Tess did not watch him go. She walked on alone until she reached her parents' house. She went inside the cottage and saw her mother coming down the stairs. It was very early in the morning, and her father, brothers and sisters were still in their beds.

'Tess!' her mother said, kissing her. 'How are you? Are you going to be married to your cousin?'

'No, mother,' Tess said. 'Alec d'Urberville is not going to marry me.'

Her mother looked closely at her daughter's face. 'You haven't told me everything.'

So Tess told her mother that the d'Urbervilles of Trantridge were not members of their family. Alec's father was called Stokes and he had taken their name – d'Urberville – for himself. Then Tess told her mother what had happened on The Chase four months ago. She told her how Alec had made love to her on that dark, foggy night.

Joan Durbeyfield listened. Then she said, 'And you've not made him marry you? Any woman would do that!'

'Perhaps any woman except me.'

'Didn't you think about us – the Durbeyfields? The d'Urbervilles could help us.'

'Should I make Alec d'Urberville marry me?' thought Tess. 'He has never spoken about marriage. And if he does? Then my answer will be "No!" I've never loved him and I don't love him now. I don't hate him, but I won't marry him.'

'Why did you let Mr d'Urberville make love to you?' asked her mother suddenly.

'Oh, mother!' said Tess. 'I was a child when I left this house four months ago! I was an innocent young girl. Why didn't you tell me about the dangers that I would find in the world? Why didn't you warn[47] me about men?'

That afternoon, some of the village girls came to visit Tess. Laughing and talking with her friends made Tess feel happier. But the next morning she lay in bed and thought about her future. She was no longer a maiden. Who would marry her now?

'I want to die,' she thought.

One Sunday morning, a few weeks later, Tess went to the church in Marlott. She loved to hear the hymns[48] and to sit quietly while the parson said the prayers. She sat in a seat at the back of the church. But people turned their heads to look at her and they began whispering about her. Tess knew that she could not come to the church again. The villagers had heard what had happened to Tess.

———

It was now August. Although it was early in the morning, the hot, bright sun shone down on the field of corn where a group of men and women worked. They were harvesting the corn that had been growing in the field all summer. The harvesting machine was cutting the stalks of corn and the farm workers were picking up the stalks and tying them into bundles.

The men and women wore hats to protect[49] their heads and faces from the strong sun. They wore gloves to protect their hands from the sharp stalks of the corn. One young woman wore a pink jacket. She was the prettiest girl working the field, but her bonnet[50] almost hid her face. Every thirty minutes she stopped working and rested. Then when she had made sure that her hat was straight on her head, she started working again.

The young woman was Tess Durbeyfield. Since Tess had returned to Marlott from Trantridge, she had changed and her life had changed. She now had a child, and she was working in the fields to earn a little money.

Tess and the other farm workers made corn bundles all morning. At eleven o'clock, a group of children came over the hill and down into the field. The eldest girl carried a baby in her arms. Another child was carrying some food and drink. The men and women stopped working and sat on the ground to eat their meal.

Tess sat a few feet away from the others. She called to the girl, who was her sister Liza-Lu, and took the baby from her. Then Tess opened her dress and began to feed her baby.

The baby finished feeding and Tess played with him for a little time. Then she began kissing him. She kissed him so many times that he began to cry.

Liza-Lu took the baby home again and Tess and the other workers continued harvesting until it was almost dark.

When they had finished working, the harvesters rode home on a large wagon. As the horses slowly pulled the heavy wagon along the road, the farm workers sang songs about the harvest.

———

When Tess reached home, she discovered that her baby was very ill.

The child had always been small and weak, but Tess was shocked[51] that he was so ill now. Then she remembered that her baby had not been baptised[52] in a church. The baby boy would go to hell if he died before a priest welcomed him into a Christian church.

Tess asked her father if the parson could come to the

She kissed him so many times that he began to cry.

house, but Jack Durbeyfield refused[53]. He would not let any of the children go and get the priest.

'No. I'll not let any parson come inside my house,' he said. 'I don't want him to know how my daughter has been ruined[54]. I don't want the parson to know about this family's shame!' And he locked the door.

During the night, Tess's son became weaker and weaker. The baby was dying. Tess walked up and down the room, praying for her child. Suddenly, she had an idea.

'Perhaps my baby *can* be saved from hell,' she thought.

She lit a candle and filled a bowl with water. Then she woke her little sisters and brothers. She made them go down onto their knees to pray.

'Are you going to baptise the baby yourself?' asked Liza-Lu. 'What are you going to call him?'

Tess had not thought about that, but now a name came into her head.

'Sorrow,' she said. 'I'm going to name my son Sorrow. Sorrow, I baptise you.' Then she put some water on the child's head. She spoke the rest of the words that she could remember of the Christian baptism ceremony.

In the morning, the child – Sorrow – died.

4

Angel Clare

Three years passed. Tess was now a beautiful twenty-year-old woman. She stayed at her father's house during the winter months. She made clothes for her sisters and brothers. In the spring, summer and autumn months, she went to work on farms to earn a little money. But Tess knew that she could never again be comfortable or happy in Marlott. It was the place where her family had tried to become members of the rich d'Urberville family. It was also the place where all the villagers knew about Tess's shame. She had to get away.

One day, early in May, a letter arrived for Mrs Durbeyfield. A friend of Mrs Durbeyfield had some news. A dairy farmer needed an extra dairymaid for the summer months. The dairy farm was called Talbothays. It was in the Vale of Frome, near land that had once belonged to the d'Urbervilles.

And so, on a sunny morning, Tess left her home for the second time. She walked to Stourcastle. Then a farmer took her in a cart to Weatherbury. Here she had a meal, then she started walking again. She arrived at Talbothays Dairy farm at four o'clock.

It was the time in the afternoon when the cows were milked[55]. Tess followed the cows as they walked through the fields to the milking-sheds. The dairymaids and dairymen came out of the buildings around the dairy yard.

May was a busy time of the year and the head dairyman, Richard Crick, was glad to see Tess.

'Can you milk well, girl?' he asked. 'Can you work hard?'

'Oh, yes,' said Tess.

'Well, you'll sleep in the dairy-house,' Head Dairyman Crick told her. 'Do you want some tea and something to eat after your long journey?'

'No, I'll begin milking now,' said Tess.

'Very well,' said Mr Crick.

Tess sat on a milking-stool and began to milk one of the cows. Soon the milk from the cow was pouring through her fingers into the bucket.

Talbothays was a large dairy farm with more than ninety red and white cows. The farm was in the Vale of Frome – a green and fertile[56] valley near the village of Mellstock. The good grass, and the clean water from the river which ran

Tess sat on a milking-stool and began to milk one of the cows.

through the valley, made the cows fat and healthy. Their milk was very good.

'The cows are giving their milk slowly today. Let's sing to them!' Mr Crick said. 'We'll get more milk.'

So the dairymen and dairymaids began to sing.

One of the men worked more slowly than all the other dairy workers.

'Milking makes my fingers tired,' he said.

The man who said these words wore a dairyman's white apron[57] over his brown trousers and his brown jacket. But he did not look and speak like the other farm workers.

'He is a gentleman,' Tess thought. 'He is well educated. Where have I seen him before?' Then she remembered. 'He stopped to dance with some of the girls at the May Dance in Marlott!'

For a moment, she was worried. Did the man recognize[58] her? He might have heard her story. But he did not remember her.

Three other dairymaids slept in the dairy-house with Tess. They were Izz Huett, Retty Priddle and Marian. The other men and women went back to their homes in the village of Mellstock each evening. Tess did not see the gentleman at supper, and she did not ask about him. By the time that they had finished their meal it was dark. Tess was very tired and she went to bed.

She was almost asleep, when one of the other dairymaids said, 'That new man is Mr Angel Clare. He's slow because he's learning to milk. He's the son of the priest at Emminster. His brothers are going to be priests and ...'

But Tess did not hear anything more. She was asleep.

———

Angel Clare was twenty-six years old. He was tall and slim with long arms and legs. He had dark eyelashes around his light blue eyes. His hair was blond and his beard was dark golden brown. Angel was the youngest son of Reverend James Clare, a priest who lived in Emminster, in the north of the county. Angel's parents wanted him to be a priest like his brothers, but Angel wanted to be a farmer. His parents were both angry and disappointed about this.

Angel Clare was going to work at Talbothays Dairy for six months. At first he stayed in his room on the top floor of the dairy-house in the evenings. He read books or played his harp[59]. But soon he came to eat his supper with Head Dairyman Crick and his wife, and the other workers. Angel enjoyed laughing and talking with these simple, country people. He also enjoyed working outside. He liked to watch the birds, the clouds in the sky, and the changing seasons[60].

At breakfast one morning, Angel heard Tess talking with the other girls. He looked up from the book that he was reading. He watched Tess for several minutes.

'What a lovely, innocent country girl!' he thought. 'But have I seen her somewhere before?'

He could not remember. But he began to watch Tess more often than he watched the other pretty dairymaids.

———

On a warm evening in June, Tess went into the garden beside the dairy yard. Everything was quiet, except for the sound of Angel Clare's harp. He was playing a beautiful, sad tune. Tess stopped and listened to the music for a moment. Then she walked slowly through the long grass, moving closer to the wall of the dairy-house. The flowers in the wet grass made red spots[61] on the skirt of her dress.

When Angel had finished playing, he put down the harp and walked into the garden. He saw Tess before she had time to move away.

'Don't go, Tess,' he said. 'Are you afraid?'

She blushed. 'No, sir,' she said. 'I'm not afraid of things that I can see and understand.'

43

'What *are* you afraid of?' he asked. 'Are you afraid of life itself?'

'Yes, sir,' said Tess.

'So am I. I'm often afraid of life,' he said. 'Sometimes, life can be difficult and serious. But why is life difficult and serious for a young girl like you?'

Tess thought for a moment. 'The trees and the rivers have eyes that watch me,' she said. 'They know what will happen in my future. And I think that I can see all my tomorrows in a line. The tomorrows are clear at first but they get smaller and smaller. I see cruel times and danger in my future. But you are lucky. You can make dreams with your music. You can drive bad thoughts away.'

'It is interesting that this young woman has these sad ideas,' thought Angel Clare.

'It is strange that this well-educated young man finds life sad and difficult,' Tess thought.

Each young person was puzzled[62] by the other. They waited to find out more about each other.

One day, Angel saw Tess looking sad.

'What's the matter?' he asked.

'I've wasted[63] my life,' she said. 'I know nothing. I've done nothing. You know so much, and I know so little. What a *nothing* I am! My past and my future are like the past and future of thousands of others like me.'

'What do you want to learn?' asked Angel.

'One thing,' replied Tess, very quietly. 'Why does the sun shine on good people and bad people in the same way?'

Then she thought for a few moments. 'He must think that I'm stupid,' Tess said to herself. 'Perhaps I'll tell him about my family – the d'Urbervilles. Perhaps if he knows that my family is old and noble, he'll think that I'm a better person.'

Later, she spoke to Mr Crick. 'Is Mr Clare interested in

the history of old and noble families?' she asked.

'No,' Mr Crick said. 'He's not like his parents and his brothers. He hates old families.'

So Tess said nothing about her ancestors.

5

'I Can Never Marry You!'

That summer, Tess and Angel watched each other all the time. As the weather became warmer, their feelings for each other became stronger. Both young people were almost in love with each other. Angel and Tess were on the edge of love, but not yet lovers. They met often because they worked together. Angel thought that Tess was more like a queen than a milkmaid.

One night, Tess was lying in her bed. The other three girls who shared[64] the room were standing by the window. Marian, Izz and Retty were watching someone in the garden. It was Angel Clare.

'It's stupid to be in love with him, Retty Priddle,' said Marian. 'He's thinking about somebody else. Oh, but I would marry him tomorrow!'

'So would I!' cried Izz Huett.

'And me,' said Retty.

'But none of *us* will marry Angel Clare. He likes Tess Durbeyfield the best,' whispered Marian. 'I've watched him every day, and it's true. He only looks at her.'

They thought about this for several minutes, then Izz Huett spoke again.

'This is foolish! He won't marry Tess, or any of us. We are simple, country girls. He is the son of a gentleman.'

They watched Angel for a few more minutes, then got

45

into their beds. Marian was soon asleep and dreaming. But Izz lay awake for a long time. She was thinking about Angel. And Retty Priddle cried until she fell asleep.

Tess could not sleep after she heard the girls' words. She knew that Angel Clare liked her more than the other girls. Tess was the youngest dairymaid, and she was prettiest. Also, she had heard Angel talking to Head Dairyman Crick.

'A country woman is the only suitable wife for a farmer,' Angel Clare had said. 'I don't think that a fine lady would be a suitable farmer's wife.'

'But one of the other girls might be suitable,' thought Tess. 'Retty, Marian or Izz might be a good wife for a young gentleman farmer. I cannot marry. I'll never marry.'

———

In the hot weather of July there were sudden storms and rain fell heavily. One Sunday morning, after they had milked the cows, Tess, Izz, Retty and Marian walked along the road to Mellstock Church.

The church was three or four miles away from Talbothays Dairy. The girls had been walking for several miles. Now they reached the lowest part of the road and found a flood there. Rainwater had run down the road and now a big pool of water was lying at the bottom of the hill.

The four girls stood and looked at the pool. They could not walk through the water. They were wearing their best white stockings[65] and thin shoes.

Suddenly, Angel Clare came round a bend[66] in the road in front of them. He walked through the pool in his long boots, and came towards the girls.

'Are you trying to get to the church?' he asked. 'I'll carry each of you over the water. Marian, I'll carry you first. Put your arms around my shoulders!'

He lifted Marian into his arms and carried her across the water. Then he came back for Izz. After he had taken Izz

'Now for the most beautiful of the four,' he said, and he picked
her up in his arms.

across the pool, he returned for Retty. But as he picked up Retty Priddle, he looked at Tess.

When he came back for Tess, he spoke quietly to her.

'Now for the most beautiful of the four,' he said, and he picked her up in his arms.

Tess looked down. She could not look into Angel's bright blue eyes. But she was excited to be so close to him.

Angel walked slowly. He took as long as possible to go through the water. At last, he put her down on dry ground at the other side of the flood. Tess's friends were watching, and she knew that they had been talking about her.

Angel quickly said goodbye and hurried back along the flooded road.

The four dairymaids walked on towards the church. Then Marian said, 'He likes you best, Tess. He wanted to kiss you!'

'No, no!' Tess said. But she knew now that she truly[67] loved Angel Clare.

'He's not thinking of marriage,' she went on. 'And if he asked me, I would say no. I cannot marry any man.'

_____

Each day, the heat of the summer sun grew stronger. And each day, Angel Clare's love for the beautiful and silent Tess grew stronger. The rain no longer fell and the weather got warmer and warmer. The dairymaids and dairymen no longer milked the cows inside the milking-sheds. They milked the cows in the fields, where it was cooler.

One afternoon, Angel and Tess were separated from the other dairy workers. They were milking cows who were in fields further from all the others. Tess was milking her favourite golden brown cow beside a hedge. She saw Angel Clare watching her. She pretended[68] that she had not noticed him looking at her. But suddenly Angel jumped up from his milking-stool and ran across to her. He dropped down onto his knees and put his arms around her.

'Oh, Tess!' he whispered. 'I love you!'

Tess tried to move away, and her eyes filled with tears.

'Why are you crying, my darling?' he asked.

'Oh – I don't know!' she said.

'Well, now you know how I feel,' said Angel. 'I love you dearly and truly. But I'll not say or do any more at this time. I have surprised you. And I have surprised myself!'

Angel let Tess go and each of them went back to their work. Nobody had seen Angel hold Tess in his arms. But from that moment, their lives were changed for ever.

That evening, Angel went and sat on the gate of the dairy yard to think. In less than six months he would be leaving Talbothays. Then, after working for a short time on some other farms, he would be ready to start work on his own farm.

His wife – a farmer's wife – should be someone who understood farming.

———

Angel decided to go and talk to his family, so he left the dairy the next morning and rode to Emminster.

When he reached the church at Emminster, Angel stopped his horse. There was a group of girls outside the church and Angel knew one of them. She was Mercy Chant, the daughter of his father's good friend. Angel's parents hoped that one day Angel would marry Mercy. But Angel could only think about Tess.

Angel's family were having breakfast when he arrived at the house. His parents and his two brothers jumped from their chairs and welcomed him. Angel was pleased to see them all, but he did not feel part of the family any more. He was more comfortable when he was with his friends on the farm.

After breakfast, Angel went for a walk with his brothers. Felix only talked about the church, and Cuthbert only spoke

49

about Cambridge University. Both of the brothers thought that farming was not a job for a gentleman.

That evening, Angel spoke to his father.

'What kind of wife do you think is best for a farmer?' he asked.

'The best wife is a good Christian woman,' Reverend Clare answered.

'It is also important that a farmer's wife can milk cows and understand how to look after animals,' said Angel.

'Yes – well, of course,' said his father. 'But you could not find a better and more truly Christian woman than Mercy Chant.'

'Yes, yes. Mercy is a good woman,' said Angel. 'But I've met someone else. And she'll be a good farmer's wife.'

'Is she like Mercy?' asked Reverend Clare. 'Is she from a good family?'

'She's not what *we* call a lady,' said Angel. 'I'm sure that her family are simple people. But she is a lady in every other way. She's a good Christian woman and she goes to church almost every Sunday. She is also honest, innocent and very beautiful.'

His parents agreed that this was good, but they told Angel not to do anything in a hurry. He must think carefully first.

––––

In the morning, Angel left Emminster and started his journey back to Talbothays. His father rode some of the way with him. Reverend Clare talked about the church and the village. Then he spoke about a young man named d'Urberville who lived in Trantridge.

'Is he one of the members of the old d'Urberville family from Kingsbere?' asked Angel.

'No, no. This is a new family who took the name. Their names used to be Stoke. The mother is a blind widow and the son is a most unpleasant young man.'

Soon after saying this, Reverend Clare returned home and Angel rode on to Talbothays.

It was afternoon when he arrived at the dairy. Everything was quiet. The workers were sleeping. Because the dairymen and women had to get up so early in the mornings, they usually slept for a few hours in the afternoons.

Angel fed his horse, then went into the silent dairy-house. It was now three o'clock and the air was hot and still. He heard a sound above him and looked up. Tess was coming down the stairs. She had left her bed earlier than the other girls. She was going to the dairy-room to make butter and cheese from the milk.

'Oh, Mr Clare!' she said. 'You frightened me! I —'

Angel put his arm around her waist. 'Dear Tess!' he said. 'Don't call me Mr Clare any more. Call me Angel.' He bent his face towards her and looked into her eyes.

She pulled away from him and walked into the dairy-room. Angel followed her and stood at her side as she moved the cool white milk in the deep metal containers.

'There's something I want to ask you,' he said. 'Soon, I shall want to marry. And I'll want a woman who knows about farming. Will you be that woman, Tess? Will you be my wife?'

Tess's face became very pale.

'Oh, Mr Clare,' she said. 'I can't be your wife!' Her eyes filled with tears.

'But Tess, don't you love me?' he asked.

'Oh, yes, yes!' she said. 'But I *cannot* marry you.'

'Have you promised to marry someone else?' asked Angel.

'No,' she said.

'Then why — ?' he began. Tess turned towards Angel.

'Your – your father is a priest, and your parents will want you to marry a lady,' said Tess. This was not the true reason, but she could not tell him the truth.

'You're wrong,' said Angel. 'I've spoken to my parents

51

'Tess, will you be my wife?'

about you. Is my proposal[69] a shock to you, my dear? I'll give you time to think before you give me an answer.'

Then Angel began to talk about other things. He talked about his parents and Emminster. He told her that his father had met an unpleasant young man who lived in Trantridge – a young man who had a blind mother.

Tess was silent as tears of anger and sadness fell from her eyes. But Angel did not notice this.

'Now, dearest Tess,' he said. 'Do you have an answer to my proposal? Will you marry me?'

'Oh, no, no!' she said. 'I can *never* marry you!'

6

Mistakes

Angel Clare proposed to Tess many times during the next few days. He asked her when they were in the fields and in the dairy-room. He asked her as they walked beside the river in the evenings. He knew that Tess loved him. He could not understand why she refused to marry him.

'Oh, Tess! Why do you disappoint me?' he said. 'Tell me that you won't marry anyone else. Tell me that you'll marry me.'

And so it went on, day after day. Each time that they were alone together, Angel proposed to Tess again. And each time, she refused him. But in bed at night, she wept.

'I know that, one day, I'll say yes. I can't help it!' she thought. 'I can't let anyone else have him! But this is wrong. And when he knows the truth, it may kill him.'

One afternoon, Angel Clare had to drive the wagon to the railway station. He had to make sure that the churns of milk were put on the train to London. He asked Tess to go with him and she agreed.

The sky was dark and it was raining when Tess and Angel started their journey back to the dairy. Tess moved closer to Angel, and they covered themselves with a large piece of cloth.

'Your heart belongs to me, Tess,' he said. 'You love me. You know that this is true. So why won't you marry me?'

'I – I've something to tell you,' she said. 'It is something about my past life.'

'Then tell me, my darling,' he said.

'I was born in Marlott, and I grew up there,' said Tess. 'But I'm ...'

'Yes?' he said.

'I'm not a Durbeyfield,' said Tess. 'I'm a d'Urberville.'

'A d'Urberville!' said Angel. 'Is that all that is worrying you? I will not love you less because you are a d'Urberville.'

'Dairyman Crick said that you hated old, noble families,' said Tess.

Angel laughed. 'Not really. I just think that it is wrong to believe that noble people are more *important* than anyone else. Is that your terrible secret? You are a d'Urberville? Well, now I know it and you have no reason to refuse me. Marry me and you'll take my name and escape from yours!'

'If you marry me, will you be happy? Are you *sure* about that?' asked Tess.

'Yes, dearest, of course!' Angel said. Then he dropped the horse's reins[70], held her and kissed her.

'Then, yes,' she said. 'I will marry you.' And immediately she began to cry.

'Why are you crying?' he asked.

'I'm happy, but – I made a promise to myself. I promised that I would die unmarried,' said Tess. 'Oh, sometimes I wish that I had never been born!'

'How can you say that, if you truly love me?' said Angel.

'But I do love you!' she cried. And she threw her arms around him and kissed him on the lips. 'There, *now* do you believe me?'

'Yes,' he said, smiling. 'I believe you.'

'I must write to my mother,' said Tess.

'Of course,' said Angel. 'Where does she live?'

'In Marlott, on the northern side of Blackmoor Vale.'

'Ah, then I *have* seen you before.'

'Yes, at the May Dance four years ago. You wouldn't dance with me,' said Tess. 'Oh, I hope that isn't bad luck for us now.'

———

Tess wrote a letter to her mother, telling her that she was engaged[71]. By the end of the week, Tess received a reply:

Dear Tess,

I hope that you are well. We are all glad to hear the news about your marriage. Don't say anything to Mr Clare about your past trouble. It was not your fault. Remember your promise to me. Do not tell anyone, ever.

We send our love to you and your young man,
Mother.

So Tess did not talk about her time at Trantridge. She did not tell Angel about the night at The Chase with Alec d'Urberville. And she did not tell Angel about the baby. She tried to forget the past, but it was not easy.

One day she cried out to Angel, 'Oh, why didn't you stay at the May Dance, when I was sixteen?'

'I wish that I had stayed on that day,' he said. 'But why do *you* wish it so strongly?'

Tess quickly tried to hide her feelings[72]. 'I would have had more years of your love,' she said.

After this, Tess and Angel were together often. They went for long walks and talked about the future. They told

Richard Crick and his wife about their plans. They decided that the date for their wedding would be 31st December.

'I'm to be Angel's wife!' Tess said to herself, as the day came nearer. 'Can it ever happen?'

———

On 24th December – Christmas Eve – Tess and Angel went shopping together in Weatherbury. After they had finished shopping, Tess waited while Angel went to get the horse and carriage.

As Tess waited in the street, two men went past. They looked at her.

'She's a lovely maiden,' the first man said.

'She's lovely, that is true,' said the second man, whose name was Farmer Groby. 'But she's not a maiden.'

At that moment, Angel returned and heard the men speaking. Angrily, he jumped from the carriage and hit the second man on the chin.

'I – I'm sorry, sir,' said Groby. He looked again at Tess. 'I made a mistake.'

After a moment, Angel said, 'All right. Perhaps I got angry too quickly. I should not have hit you.'

Angel gave the man some money and drove away with Tess. The two men continued walking along the street.

'*Did* you make a mistake?' asked the first man.

'No, I didn't,' said Groby. 'She's not a maiden.'

After this, Tess decided to tell Angel the truth. But she did not know how to speak to him about it. So she decided to write him a letter. In the letter she told him about Alec D'urberville and the baby, Sorrow. When she had finished writing the letter, she pushed it under the door of Angel's room.

Tess slept badly that night. The next morning, Angel came down from his room and kissed her, but he said nothing about the letter. Had he read it? Perhaps he had forgiven[73] her.

56

'I – I'm sorry, sir,' said Groby. 'I made a mistake.'

———

Every morning and night for the next few days, Angel was the same. He kissed Tess and told her many times that he loved her. But he said nothing about the letter. At last it was their wedding day. Tess's family and friends were not coming to the wedding because they lived too far away. Angel had written to his family. He had told them of the time and date of his wedding. His brothers had not replied, but his parents wrote a sad letter. It said: *We are sorry that you are hurrying into marriage. But you are old enough to decide who you should marry.*

Angel was not upset by this message. He planned to visit his parents with Tess soon. He could tell them that she was a d'Urberville when he saw them. They would be pleased to know that Tess came from an old, noble family.

Tess thought again about her letter to Angel. Had he found it? She left her breakfast and went up the stairs to his room. And there she found the letter, just inside his door. The letter had gone under the carpet. He had never seen it!

Tess's hands were shaking with fear as she picked up the envelope. She could not let Angel see the letter now. It was too late. Everyone was busy getting ready for the wedding.

A little later, Tess saw Angel when he was alone.

'I want to tell you all about my mistakes, Angel!' she said.

'Don't tell me today, my dear,' said Angel. 'There will be plenty of time later to tell me about all your mistakes. And then I can tell you about mine!'

'You truly don't want me to tell you, my love?' she said.

'I do not, Tess – really,' he said.

———

Only Mr Crick, his wife, and a few other people came to the wedding in Mellstock Church. After the ceremony, Angel and Tess went back to Talbothays. It was raining and Tess was tired and unhappy.

58

'I am now married. I'm Mrs Angel Clare,' she thought. 'Or is this the real truth? Am I really Mrs Alec d'Urberville? I became Alec's wife when we were together in The Chase. There was no marriage ceremony for us, but Alec d'Urberville was the father of my dead child.'

Tess and Angel left Talbothays later that afternoon and drove along the Vale of Frome to Wellbridge. Before they reached Wellbridge, they turned and drove the horse and carriage over the stone bridge that gave the village its name. Immediately past the bridge was the manor house where Angel and Tess were going to stay for a few days. It was the house where some members of the old d'Urberville family had lived many years ago.

Inside the house, on the walls beside the stairs, there were portraits of d'Urberville women. Each picture showed a proud, middle-aged woman with a thin nose and sharp bright eyes.

Angel and Tess walked up the stairs to the sitting-room. On a table in the sitting-room there was a parcel. Inside it there was a letter and a box made of fine leather. The letter was from Angel's father.

Dear Son,

You will remember that these jewels were given to you when you were fifteen. They have been kept until today – your wedding day. We are sending them to you now so that you can give them to your wife.

Father

Inside the box, there were earrings, bracelets and a necklace. They were all made of diamonds. Angel held them up against Tess's beautiful pale skin. He smiled and helped her to put on the jewellery. Tess's grey-blue eyes and the bright diamonds shone in the light of the candles.

'How beautiful you are!' he whispered, and he kissed her.

After Tess and Angel had eaten supper, Jonathan Kail, a

Tess's grey-blue eyes and the bright diamonds shone in the light of the candles.

dairyman from Talbothays, arrived with their luggage.

'I'm sorry that I'm late, Mr Clare,' Jonathan said. 'But something terrible happened after you left. Retty Priddle tried to drown[74] herself!'

'Oh!' cried Tess.

'Retty and Marian went to drink at several inns before they returned home,' said Jonathan. 'Later, someone found Retty in the river, but she wasn't dead. Another person found Marian sleeping in a field!'

'And Izz?' asked Tess. 'What happened to Izz Huett?'

'Izz is at the dairy, but she's very unhappy,' said Jonathan. Then he said goodbye and left the house.

Tess went into the bedroom and lit the fire while Angel brought the luggage into the room. Outside, it was raining and the evening was cold.

'I'm sorry that you had to hear that sad story about the girls,' he said.

Tess did not reply. She watched the bright flames in the fireplace.

'They're innocent girls who only want to be loved,' Tess thought. 'I have Angel's love, but *I* am not innocent. It was wrong of me to take Angel's love and say nothing. I must tell Angel everything. I must tell him the truth about my life.'

Angel held Tess's hand and looked into her eyes.

'This morning we both wanted to talk about our mistakes,' he said suddenly. 'Perhaps now is the time for me to tell you *my* mistake. I want you to forgive me.'

'Angel, I'm sure that I will forgive you!' said Tess.

'When I was in London a few years ago, I met a woman – a stranger,' said Angel. 'I stayed with her for two days and I made love to her. But then I realized that the relationship was very wrong, and I came home. I've never done anything like that again. Do you forgive me, Tess?'

'Oh, Angel, I am glad that you have told me this!' said

Tess. 'Because *I've* made a mistake and now *you* can forgive *me*.'

'Then tell me your story,' said Angel. 'It cannot be a more serious mistake than mine.'

'No!' she said, happily. 'It isn't more serious than yours!'

Tess sat by the fire, held Angel's hand, and told him the story of her life at The Slopes. She told Angel about her meeting with Alec d'Urberville, and what happened on The Chase. As she spoke, the light from the fire threw Tess's shadow[75] high up onto the wall of the bedroom.

7

Angel Goes Away

Tess finished her story and Angel stood up. His face was pale. He could not look at her.

'Tess,' he said. 'Can I believe this? Is it true, or are you mad? You don't *seem* to be mad.' He stopped for a moment, then sat down again. 'Why didn't you tell me before?' he said. 'Oh, but I stopped you, I remember now.'

Tess knelt on the floor next to Angel's feet. The fire was burning brightly but she did not feel warm. Suddenly she felt cold and afraid. 'Please, forgive me,' she whispered. When he did not answer, she said, '*I* forgive *you*, Angel.'

'You – yes, you do,' he said.

'But don't you forgive *me*?' she said.

'This changes everything,' said Angel sadly. 'Tess, I believed that you were a good, honest, innocent woman. Now I know that you are not these things. The woman that I loved is not you.'

Tess's face became white with fear and she began to cry. 'Don't – don't I belong to you any more?'

Angel watched her and waited for her to stop weeping.

'I – I won't ask you to let me live with you,' Tess said. 'I cannot ask you to do that. And I won't write to my family and tell them that we're married. I'll only do the things that you order me to do. If you go away from me, I'll not follow you. If you never speak to me again, I won't ask why.'

'Tess,' said Angel, gently but politely. 'I cannot stay here. I'm going out to walk a little way.' And he quietly left the room.

After he closed the door, Tess jumped up. Quickly, she pulled on her coat and followed him.

The rain had stopped falling and the night sky was clear now. Angel went over the bridge in front of the house, along the road, and through the fields. After several hours of heavy rain, there were now pools of water on the road and the fields. After a few minutes, Tess was walking next to her husband.

'I still love you, Angel!' she said. 'I was a child when Alec d'Urberville took me to The Chase. I knew nothing about men.'

'What happened was that man's fault, not yours. I know that,' said Angel.

'Then will you forgive me?' she said.

'I do forgive you, but that is not enough,' he said.

'Do you love me, Angel?' Tess asked.

He did not answer.

'Oh, Angel!' said Tess. 'My mother says that these things happen sometimes. Often the husband forgives his wife. And those wives don't love their husbands as much as I love you!'

'You're a simple country girl. You do not understand —' began Angel.

'I'm a d'Urberville!' said Tess.

'It would be better if you *weren't* a d'Urberville!' he said. 'It would be better if you *were* a simple country girl.'

63

They walked on silently. Then Tess said, 'What can I do to end your sadness? The river is down there. Shall I drown myself in it?'

'I don't want to add your death to my other mistakes,' he said. 'Go back to the house and go to bed.'

'All right, I will,' said Tess.

Later that night, Angel Clare returned to the house. He found Tess sleeping peacefully upstairs in the bedroom. He was going to lie beside her on the bed, but then he noticed a picture on the wall. It was the portrait of a d'Urberville woman, one of Tess's ancestors.

'She is not a pleasant-looking woman,' Angel thought. 'She's a woman who would betray[76] a man.'

This thought made him turn away from the bed. He went downstairs to sleep alone in the sitting-room.

———

At breakfast the next morning, Angel said, 'Tess! Tell me that your story isn't true!'

'It is true,' she replied.

'Every word?' said Angel.

'Every word.'

'Is the baby alive?'

'He died,' said Tess.

'And the – the man?' Angel could not say the name of the man who had destroyed his happiness[77].

'He's alive.'

'Is he in England?' Angel asked.

'Yes,' she said.

Angel stood up and began to walk around the room, thinking.

'Angel,' she said. 'You – you can divorce[78] me.'

'Divorce! How can you be so stupid?' he said. 'I cannot divorce you.'

'Can't you divorce me, now that I've told you everything?'

'Tess, you're like a child!' he said. 'You don't understand the law.'

'I'll kill myself. Then you'll be free,' said Tess.

He was shocked. 'You must never think of doing that!'

'Then *you* should kill me!' she said. 'It's the only way that you can escape from your marriage to me.'

'Don't say that!' he said.

They finished their breakfast. Then Angel went out to work at a mill near Wellbridge. His work at the mill was part of his farming studies. It was the reason that they had come to stay in the area. That evening Angel studied, and the next morning he got up early to go the mill again.

'Goodbye, Tess,' he said.

Tess held her face up so that he could kiss her, but Angel walked away.

———

Tess and Angel continued like this for another day. They were living in the same house, but they were not together. Tess slept in the bedroom and Angel slept in the sitting-room. They did not share a bed. Tess did not expect Angel to forgive her. More than once, she thought about leaving while he was at the mill.

During this time, Angel Clare thought carefully about the future.

'What can we do?' he said to himself. 'What can we do?'

Then, the next evening, Tess said, 'You are not going to live with me for very long, are you, Angel?'

'I can't,' he said. 'How can I live with you? How can we live together while that man is alive? Think of the future. If we have children and they find out the truth, they will be shamed. And they *will* find out the truth. People who know your story will tell them.'

'You're right,' said Tess. 'I cannot ask you to stay with me. You must go away.'

65

'But what will you do?' he asked.

'I'll go home,' she said. 'I'll go to Marlott tomorrow.'

'And I won't stay here,' Angel said. 'I think kinder thoughts about people when I'm away from them. Perhaps we can be together again one day.'

The next morning, after breakfast, Angel and Tess left the manor house in a hired carriage. They travelled together for several miles, then Angel got out of the carriage.

'Please understand,' he said to Tess. 'I'm not angry with you, but I cannot live with you now. I'll tell you where I'm going as soon as I know. I'll visit you when I can, Tess. But don't try to find me.'

'Can I write to you?' she asked.

'Oh, yes. If you're ill, or if you want anything, write to me,' he said. 'But I expect that I'll write to you first.'

'I'll agree to this because you know what is best,' said Tess.

She made it easy for Angel. She did not cry or shout out. Angel gave her some money, then he said goodbye. He watched the carriage go away down the road and climb up the hill.

He hoped that Tess would look back at him. But she did not, so he walked on. He did not realize that he still loved her.

————

Mrs Durbeyfield was washing clothes when her daughter arrived home.

'Tess!' she said. 'I thought that you were married!'

'Yes, mother, I am,' said Tess.

'Then where is your husband?' asked Joan Durbeyfield.

'Oh, he's gone away for a while,' said Tess.

'Gone away! When were you married?'

'Tuesday, mother,' replied Tess. 'New Year's Eve.'

'But today is only Saturday,' said Mrs Durbeyfield. 'You have only been married for five days. Why has he gone away?'

Tess went across to her mother. She put her head on her mother's arm, and began to cry.

'Mother, you told me that I must not tell Angel about my past. But I did! And he went away.'

'Oh, Tess! You fool!' said Mrs Durbeyfield. 'You little fool!'

'I know. I know that I'm a fool! But he was so good to me. I had to tell him the truth.'

'But you married your husband before you told him!' said her mother.

'Yes,' said Tess. 'If he couldn't forgive me, he could divorce me. That is what I thought. But I didn't understand the law. And oh, you don't know how much I love him! I wanted to marry him more than anything!'

'What will you father say?' said her mother. 'He's been telling everyone at Rolliver's and the Pure Drop Inn about your wedding. You've helped the Durbeyfields to find their noble ancestors. And now you've done this!'

Suddenly they heard Tess's father coming towards the house. He was singing. Mrs Durbeyfield told Tess to go upstairs.

'Stay up there until I've told him the bad news,' she said.

So Tess went up to her bedroom. But she could hear every word that her mother said to her father. Mrs Durbeyfield told her husband about Tess's wedding. And she told him that Angel Clare had gone away.

Jack Durbeyfield was angry.

'What will people say, Joan?' he cried. 'They'll laugh at me at the Pure Drop and at Rolliver's! I shall kill myself! Did Angel Clare *really* marry Tess?'

Poor Tess could not listen anymore. She covered her ears with her hands. If her family did not believe her, what would people in the village think? No, she could not stay in Marlott for long.

67

After a few days, Tess received a note from Angel Clare. His message told her that he had gone to the north of England, to look at a farm. Tess told her mother that she was going to meet Angel. She gave Joan Durbeyfield half the money that Angel had given her. Then she left Marlott.

―――――

Three weeks after his marriage, Angel Clare returned to Emminster to see his parents. He had tried to continue with his plans to become a farmer, but he had become tired and worried. Tess was – or had been – part of his plans. He had wanted to share his life with her. Perhaps he had been cruel to her.

Perhaps he should forgive her – forget her past. Should they go to another country, where no one would know them? He had heard that Brazil was a good country for farming. They could live peacefully there.

Angel's parents were surprised to see him.

'Where is your wife, Angel?' asked Mrs Clare.

'She's at her mother's home for a short time,' said Angel. 'I've come home quickly because I've decided to go to Brazil.'

'Brazil!' repeated his parents. They were surprised to hear this news but they wanted to know more about their son's marriage.

'Three weeks ago we received your note telling us about your wedding,' Mrs Clare said. 'Why have we never met your wife? You did not want to get married here, or at the church in her village. You decided to marry her at the dairy farm. So we did not come to the wedding. But we're not angry, and we want to meet your wife. Why don't you bring her here? What has happened?'

'She's staying with her parents. She'll stay there while I go to Brazil,' said Angel. 'I cannot take her with me on my first journey there. You'll meet her before we both go to live in Brazil. I'll bring her here, to Emminster.'

'And is she a good, innocent girl? A maiden?'

Angel and his parents ate supper, and Angel told them more about his plans. But his mother was still disappointed that she had not met Tess.

'I'm sure that she's very pretty, Angel,' she said.

'Yes, she is,' he said. 'She's beautiful.'

'And is she a good, innocent girl? A maiden?'

'Yes, of course, mother,' Angel replied.

'And you were her first love?' asked Mrs Clare.

'Yes, I was,' he said.

'Well, you're going to be a farmer. Perhaps it is a good thing that your wife is a country girl,' said his mother. 'I wish that I could have met this beautiful, innocent girl who loves you, Angel. But I'm so happy for you.'

Angel's eyes filled with tears. He said goodnight quickly and went to his bedroom. But his mother followed him and knocked on his door. Angel opened it and saw her standing outside. She was worried.

'Angel, why are you going away so soon?' she asked. 'Is something wrong? Is there trouble with Tess? There is! Is – is she a woman with secrets? Has she made ... mistakes?'

'She is a good girl!' said Angel.

'Then the rest doesn't matter,' his mother said. 'There's nothing more beautiful than a young, innocent country girl.'

Once again, Angel became angry with Tess. He had told a lie to his parents because of her. But then he remembered Tess's soft voice and the touch of her warm red lips. He remembered her pale skin, dark hair and grey-blue eyes. He could not be angry for long.

Before he left Wessex, Angel went to the manor house in Wellbridge where he and Tess had stayed after their wedding. He had to collect some things that they had left there. He stood in front of the house that had been the home of the old and noble d'Urberville family. After a few minutes, tears began to run down his face.

'Oh, Tess!' he said. 'Why didn't you tell me everything before we married? I would have forgiven you.'

Suddenly, he heard a sound and he turned around. Izz Huett, the dairymaid, was standing behind him.

'Mr Clare,' said the young woman. 'I've come to see you and Mrs Clare.'

'Here is an honest young girl who loved me,' Angel thought. 'This girl would have been a good farmer's wife. She would have been as suitable as Tess.'

'I'm here alone,' he said to Izz. 'Tess and I are not living here now. I'm leaving England, Izz. I'm going to Brazil.'

'And I'm not living at Talbothays,' said Izz. 'I – I was too unhappy there.'

'Yes, I understand,' Angel said, kindly. 'If I had asked you to marry me, Izz, what would you have said?'

'I would have said "yes",' the dairymaid replied. 'And you would have had a woman who loved you!'

'I'm going to Brazil alone, Izz,' he said. 'Tess and I are not going to be together. I may never live with her again. Will you go with me, instead of her?'

'Do you really want me to go with you?' asked Izz.

'I do,' he said. 'Do you love me very much, Izz?'

'I do!' she said. 'I loved you from the first time that I saw you at the dairy.'

'Do you love me more than Tess loved me?'

'Well ... no,' the young woman said. 'I don't love you more than Tess. Nobody could love you more than Tess. She would die for you.'

Angel was silent. His eyes filled with tears. He heard Izz's words again and again in his head. *Nobody could love you more than Tess. She would die for you.*

'Forget what I said, Izz,' he said suddenly. 'I was crazy! You are not my wife. You cannot be my wife. I cannot take you to Brazil. I'm sorry!'

71

'I was too honest!' Izz cried out, weeping. 'Oh, why did I tell you the truth!'

'You were right to tell me,' he said. 'You are a good woman, Izz, but I have a loving wife.'

'Yes, you have,' the young woman said sadly.

Angel said goodbye to Izz Huett and left Wellbridge. That night, he went to London on the train. Five days later, he began his journey by ship to Brazil.

8

'I Was Shown a Better Way!'

After leaving Marlott, Tess worked as a dairymaid. She worked in dairies during the spring and summer. Then, at harvest time, she decided to work in the fields at a farm where Marian was working. On the journey there, a man passed her on the road. He turned to look at her.

'You're the young woman who was at Weatherbury on Christmas Eve!' he said to her.

Tess recognized Farmer Groby. He was the man that Angel had knocked down on that day.

'I spoke the truth that evening, didn't I?' said Groby. 'You were not a maiden.'

Tess did not answer him. Instead, she ran along the road until she could not see Groby any more.

That night Tess slept in a field beneath some trees. In the morning, she walked on until she came to the quiet village of Flintcomb-Ash, where she met Marian.

'Tess – Mrs Clare!' said Marian. 'Are things really so bad for you? You're the wife of a gentleman. Why do you to have to work and live like this?'

72

Tess and Marian worked hard in the rain and the wind.

'It is wrong and I'm very unhappy,' said Tess. 'But please don't ask me any questions. My husband has left England. He has gone overseas and I've used all the money that he gave me. Now I have to work. Please call me Tess, not Mrs Clare.'

———

The work at Flintcomb-Ash Farm was difficult because the land was poor. The ground was full of stones and crops did not grow well there. That winter, the weather was cold. Tess and Marian worked hard in the rain and the wind. They talked about the time when they lived happily together at Talbothays Dairy.

'I'll write to Izz Huett,' said Marian. 'Perhaps she'll come here and work with us. Then we can talk about Talbothays every day. We can talk together and remember the happy time that we spent there.'

So Marian wrote to Izz, and two or three days later she received a reply.

'Izz has promised to come!' Marian told Tess.

———

Some weeks later, when there was snow on the ground, Izz Huett arrived at Flintcomb-Ash Farm. Now the three friends began to work together. One day the farmer came and spoke to them and Tess recognized him immediately. It was Farmer Groby. The man that Angel had knocked to the ground. The man who she had met on the road.

'Ha!' he said to Tess. 'You thought that you'd got away from me on the road a few weeks ago. Well, now you are working for *me*. You must do whatever I tell you to do!' And he laughed, a hard unpleasant laugh. After that day, he made the three girls work harder than any of the other workers on the farm.

Once, Tess saw Marian and Izz whispering together.

'Were you and Izz talking about my husband?' Tess asked Marian later.

'Well, yes,' said Marian. 'Izz didn't want me to tell you, but – oh, Tess! Angel asked Izz to go away to Brazil with him!'

Tess's face became as white as the snow on the fields.

'What did Izz reply to Angel?' she asked.

'I don't know,' said Marian. 'But then Angel told her to forget everything that he had said to her.'

'Then his invitation was a joke!' said Tess.

'It wasn't a joke, Tess. Oh, I wish that I hadn't told you!' said Marian.

'No, you were right to tell me,' said Tess. 'I must write to Angel. I've been waiting for him to write to me. I was wrong.'

That evening, Tess started to write a letter to Angel.

'I don't understand,' she said to herself. 'What kind of husband is Angel? He asked Izz to go with him immediately after he left me. How can I write to him and tell him that I love him now?'

She could not finish writing the letter.

'Why hasn't *he* written to *me*?' she thought. 'I'll go and see his parents in Emminster. Perhaps they have news about him.'

———

On a Sunday two weeks later, when the snow was gone, Tess left Flintcomb-Ash. She was going to walk fifteen miles to Emminster and meet Angel's family. At three o'clock in the morning, she put on her best clothes and started her journey. Marian and Izz wished her good luck and watched her go.

It was twelve months since Tess's wedding. On this dry, dark, winter morning, she hoped for just one thing. She hoped to get love and forgiveness from Angel's family. She also hoped to get help from them. Perhaps they would help her to bring Angel home.

The first part of the journey was along the edge of the Vale of Blackmoor. But as Tess got closer to Emminster, she began to feel a little afraid. She could see the church where

75

Angel's father preached and she began to wish that she had not come. Reverend Clare had a strong belief in the Christian religion. And she was travelling on a Sunday. Perhaps he would think that this was wrong. But she had to go on now.

At the top of the hill above Emminster, she took off her heavy leather boots and hid them in a hedge. She would get them later. Then she put on her pretty, thin shoes and walked down to Reverend Clare's house. She rang the bell beside the front door. Nobody came to the door, so she rang the bell again. Nobody came.

'Perhaps the family is in the church,' she thought. She went to look for a quiet place to wait.

She started to walk past the church and back up the hill. Just then, people began to come out of the church and follow her up the hill. After a minute or two, Tess heard the voices of two young men who were walking behind her. Suddenly, she recognized the voices. Angel's brothers, Felix and Cuthbert, were behind her. They were walking quickly, and in a few seconds they had passed Tess.

'There's Mercy Chant,' Felix said, pointing to a girl on the hill ahead of them. 'Poor Angel! Why didn't he marry Mercy? She's a lady! But no, our brother married a *dairymaid* – a common country girl! Why has he done this? And are he and the dairymaid living together yet?'

'I don't know,' said Cuthbert. 'Angel tells me nothing. Since his marriage, we haven't spoken to each other.'

Felix and Cuthbert walked across to Mercy Chant and the three of them began to walk up the hill together. At the top of the hill, one of the brothers saw something lying in the hedge.

'Here's a pair of old boots!' Felix said. 'How strange!'

'They're very good boots,' said Mercy Chant. 'Why has someone thrown them in the hedge? That is foolish and

76

'Here's a pair of old boots!' Felix said. 'How strange!'

wrong. I'll carry the boots home and give them to a poor person.'

Tess walked quickly past them. Tears ran down her face. She could not return to Reverend Clare's house now.

Her journey back to Flintcomb-Ash was slow. She was tired and unhappy. When she came to the village of Evershead, Tess saw a crowd of people. They were listening to the words of a preacher. Tess stood at the edge of the crowd and listened with them.

'I was once a bad, bad person,' said the preacher. 'But now, my friends, that part of my life is finished! Now I'm a good Christian, and I am sorry for my mistakes. I was shown a better way by a good priest!'

Tess put one hand up to her mouth.

'I recognize the voice of that preacher!' she thought. She moved quickly round the edge of the crowd. She wanted to see the preacher's face.

The afternoon sun shone down on the young man who was speaking. It was Alec d'Urberville.

9

A Changed Man

It was the first time that Tess had seen Alec since the day that she had left Trantridge. She saw that he was different. He was a changed man. He was now a preacher – a man who lived an honest, good life and told other people about God. He no longer had a thick black moustache. But he had long whiskers on his cheeks and he was wearing dark clothes. Alec's life was different now but Tess was still afraid of him.

Tess tried to move away before Alec saw her, but she was too late. He looked across the heads of the people in the crowd and recognized her. Suddenly his voice became quieter and he could not find the right words to say.

Tess hurried away along the road, but she knew that Alec was watching her.

'I'll *never* escape from my past,' she thought. 'There will always be something or someone to bring back the painful memories[79].'

She heard the sound of footsteps behind her. She knew that Alec was following her.

'Tess!' he called. 'It's me – Alec d'Urberville!'

She turned and looked at him. Her eyes were cold and her voice was hard. 'Yes?' she said.

'You're thinking, "Why has he followed me?" ' said Alec.

'I am,' replied Tess. 'And I wish that you hadn't followed me.'

'But, Tess, you are the person who I want to save from hell!' cried Alec. 'God and Reverend Clare of Emminster saved me. And now I want to save you. Have you heard of Mr Clare?'

'I have,' said Tess.

'Two or three years ago, Reverend Clare preached at Trantridge,' said Alec. 'He tried to save me then, but I told him to go away. Later, I began to think about the things that he said. Since then I've tried to tell others about God. I've tried to save other people from hell. It's —'

'Don't say anything more!' cried Tess. 'You have changed completely. I cannot believe this! How can you talk to me in this way? Have you forgotten that night on The Chase? Have you forgotten what you did?'

'Tess, don't say that!' said Alec. 'I'm a good Christian man now.'

'I can't believe it,' she said.

Alec and Tess came to a place where a large stone stood on the junction[80] of two roads. This was a wild and lonely place and the stone was unlike any other stone in that part of the country. People hurried past this strange stone because it made them feel uncomfortable and a little afraid.

'I must leave you here,' said Alec. 'I have to preach at Abbot's-Cernel at six o'clock this evening. You speak well now, Tess. You don't speak like a country girl. You speak like a well-educated lady. Who taught you?'

'I've learnt many things and I've had many troubles,' said Tess.

'What troubles?' he asked.

She told him about her baby, Sorrow.

'Tess!' he cried. 'Why didn't you tell me about our child? Why didn't you write to me?'

She did not reply.

'Well, you'll see me again,' Alec d'Urberville said.

'No,' said Tess. 'Don't come near me again.'

'I'll pray for you,' said Alec.

He turned right at the junction, passed the stone, and went down the road to Abbot's-Cernel. Tess watched him for a moment, then she walked the other way.

———

Several days passed. It was now February. A cold, dry, winter wind blew across the fields where Tess and her friends worked. Then one day, Tess looked up from her work and saw Alec d'Urberville walking towards her. He was wearing the black clothes of a preacher.

'I want to speak to you, Tess,' he said quietly.

'I asked you to stay away from me,' she said.

'I've got something important to tell you.'

'Then tell me.'

'Since you left Trantridge, my mother has died. The Slopes and the farm are now mine,' he said. 'But I'm going to sell them. I'm going to preach to the poor people in Africa. I want you to be my wife and I want you to come with me.'

'Oh no, sir!' said Tess quickly. 'I can't!'

'Why?' he said.

'I don't love you. I could *never* love you,' she said. 'I love somebody else.'

Alec was shocked when he heard this. 'Your love for this man might not last long. Perhaps after a time, you will love me.'

'No!' she said.

'Why not?'

'I am married to him,' said Tess.

'Oh!' he cried, and stared at her.

'It's a secret,' she said. 'No one at Flintcomb-Ash knows that I'm married. Please don't tell anybody.'

'Where is your husband?' asked Alec. 'Is he on this farm?'

'No. He's far away.'

'Far away from *you*? And he leaves you to work like *this*?' said Alec, looking at Tess's cold red hands. 'What kind of husband is he?'

'He doesn't know that I'm working here,' said Tess.

'Does he write to you?' asked Alec.

'I – I can't tell you,' she answered.

'He *doesn't* write to you,' said Alec. 'That's the truth, isn't it?' He tried to hold her hands, but she pulled them away.

'Go away from me, please!' she said.

At that moment, Farmer Groby rode across the field on his horse. He was angry when he saw Tess talking to a stranger.

'Why aren't you working?' he asked Tess angrily.

'Don't talk to her like that!' said Alec.

'Who is this man?' Groby asked Tess.

Tess looked at Alec. 'Go – please, go!' she said.

'Well, I suppose that I must do as you tell me,' said Alec. And he walked away across the field.

That night, Tess began writing another letter to Angel

81

Clare. Her words told of her great love for him. But she could not finish the letter. Angel had asked Izz to go with him to Brazil.

'Perhaps he does not love me at all,' she thought.

———

Several days later, Alec came to see Tess at the cottage where she was living.

'Tess, I have been thinking about you all the time,' he said. 'I started to go to Casterbridge this afternoon. I was going to preach there. But I had to come and see you.'

'I have a husband,' Tess said. 'You must leave.'

Alec went away, but a few weeks later, he returned to Flintcomb-Ash. He came to the field where Tess was working by the threshing machine. He was not wearing dark clothes now. He was wearing rich, fashionable clothes and he had cut the whiskers from his cheeks. Once more, he looked like a young gentleman. He stood at the edge of the field, watching her.

Izz and Marian saw Alec first.

'Who is that?' asked Izz.

'It's the preacher who comes to see Tess,' said Marian. 'He's wearing different clothes now, but it's the same man.'

'It's not right for him to visit a married woman so often,' said Izz. 'Her husband is in another country, and —'

'Oh, it's all right,' said Marian. 'Tess loves her husband. Nothing that the preacher says will change her love. But perhaps it should.'

The other workers stopped working and ate their dinner. But Tess could not stop working. She had to keep putting the corn into the threshing machine. Alec d'Urberville came to stand beside the machine and speak to Tess.

'I'm here again,' he said. 'Since you told me about the child, I think about you night and day. I see your beautiful face in my dreams. I cannot preach any more – and it's your

Tess hit Alec's face with one of her heavy leather gloves.

fault! I cannot continue my work as a preacher. You have made me feel like this. You must leave your stupid husband and come and share my life for ever!'

Angrily, Tess hit Alec's face with one of her heavy leather gloves. Blood came from his mouth and he wiped it away with a handkerchief.

'Now hit *me*!' said Tess. 'I won't cry!'

'Oh no, Tess,' he said. 'I can forgive you for this. But remember one thing!' Alec's voice became cold and cruel, and he put his hands on her shoulders. 'If you are any man's wife, you are *mine*!' He lifted his hands. His eyes were bright with anger as he looked at her. 'I'll leave you now, Tess. But I'll come back for your answer this afternoon.'

10

Three Letters

Alec came back to the field at three o'clock. Tess saw him standing under the trees. At six o'clock, when the work was finished, he met her by the gate.

'I told Groby that this work was too hard for women,' Alec said. 'I'll walk home with you.'

'Oh, very well. Walk with me if you want to,' Tess said. She was tired. 'You asked me to marry you *before* you knew about our child. Perhaps you're not *all* bad. Perhaps you can be kind sometimes.'

'If I cannot marry you, at least I can help you,' he said. 'I have enough money to help you, and your family.'

'Have you seen my family?' Tess asked quickly. 'God knows, the Durbeyfields need help! But no, no! I cannot take anything from you. I cannot take anything for them or for me.'

They walked on, and Alec left her when they reached her

cottage. After supper that night, Tess went to her room and wrote a letter to Angel.

My Dear Husband,

I'm writing to ask for help. I have nobody else that I can ask. There is someone – a man – who is watching me. I am afraid to say his name. Come to me now! Please, help me before something terrible happens. I know that you are far away. But I think that I'll die if you don't come soon. You punished[81] me and that was right. But please be kind and come to me now! I'll be happy if I can die in your arms.

Or can I come to you? If you don't want me to be your wife, I'll be your servant. I just want to see you and to be near you. I am afraid that something terrible is going to happen to me. I'm afraid that someone will trick[82] me. Oh, Angel, let me come to you now. Or please come to me!

Your Sad and Loving Wife,
Tess

The letter for Angel arrived at his father's house in Emminster a few days later.

'I think that this is a letter from Angel's wife,' Reverend Clare said to Mrs Clare. 'Angel planned to visit us at the end of next month. Perhaps this letter will bring him home more quickly.'

At this time, Angel was riding across Brazil towards the sea. He was sick, and he knew now that he could not farm in this country. Many young European men had come to Brazil. They had hoped that they would have good lives there. They had dreamt that one day they would be rich. Many had died.

Angel had thought a lot about Tess. He had thought about what had happened to her. Why had she not written to him? Had he punished Tess too quickly? Perhaps her troubles had not been her fault.

These thoughts came to Angel when Tess was staying in Flintcomb-Ash, but before she wrote to him. He had told

Tess to wait for him to write first. But he had forgotten about this.

Angel had travelled in Brazil with another Englishman. They were both unhappy and disappointed. The travellers told their troubles to each other. Angel told his friend the sad story of his marriage.

'You were wrong to leave your wife,' Angel's friend had said.

The next day, there had been a bad storm. Both men had got very wet and cold, and Angel's friend had become ill. A few days later, he died. Angel buried him, then went on alone.

The man's words stayed in Angel's head. Angel also remembered Izz Huett's words: *Nobody could love you more than Tess. She would die for you.*

Angel remembered Tess on their wedding night. She had looked at him with love in her eyes. She had not believed that he could not love her any more.

———

At Flintcomb-Ash, Tess waited for a reply to her letter. She was sure that Angel would come home to her. She began to think about things that would please him when he came home.

Then, one cold dark evening, her sixteen-year-old sister arrived at the cottage.

'Liza-Lu!' said Tess. 'What has happened? Is something wrong at home?'

'Mother is very ill,' said Liza-Lu. 'The doctor says that she's dying. Father isn't well either. He says that it's wrong for him – a man from the noble d'Urberville family – to work. Oh Tess, we don't know what to do!'

Tess thought for a moment. She decided to go home immediately. She told Liza-Lu to sleep in her bed. The younger girl was too tired to return home that night.

It was ten o'clock when Tess started her journey to Marlott. She had to walk fifteen miles. Tess thought about her mother as she walked. She did not think about the dark shadows that moved in the trees and hedges.

At three o'clock in the morning, Tess arrived in Marlott. Light from a candle was shining from the bedroom window of her parents' house.

Tess quietly opened the door and saw her father sitting in a chair by the fire. She went up the stairs. Her mother was sleeping in the bedroom. Tess went downstairs again and started to make some breakfast.

———

After that day, Mrs Durbeyfield slowly began to get well. Jack Durbeyfield was not really ill, and he had a new plan to get money for the family.

'I'm going to find all the people in the country who are interested in history,' he told Tess. 'Then I'm going to ask them for money. I'm sure that they'll be happy to give it. They give lots of money to repair old houses and church buildings. And they give money to people who find old bones under the ground. Well, *I'm* a member of a very old, noble family – the d'Urbervilles. And I'm alive! They can help *me*.'

Tess had no time to talk about this with her father. Each day, she helped her mother in the house. She washed clothes, cooked meals and looked after the children. Then in the afternoons, she went to the village allotments. Tess often worked on the family's allotment until it was nearly dark. Her sister, Liza-Lu, worked with her. The villagers pulled up the long grass, dug the ground, and planted vegetable seeds in their allotments. Later they burnt the grass in small fires. The smoke from the fires made the workers look like grey ghosts.

One evening in March, Tess sent Liza-Lu home early.

Suddenly the flames of her fire shone brightly on his face and she recognized him.

Tess continued working. As she worked, she sang a song. At first she did not notice the man working near her, and he did not speak to her. Then suddenly, the flames of her fire shone brightly on his face and she recognized him. It was Alec d'Urberville!

'Why are *you* here?' Tess asked him.

'I've come to see you, Tess,' he said. 'You shouldn't be working like this.'

'I like working here,' she said. 'I'm doing this for my father. He cannot work. And the family needs this food.'

'Have you finished your work at Flintcomb-Ash Farm?' Alec asked.

'Yes,' she replied.

'Where are you going next?' asked Alec. 'Are you going to meet your dear husband?'

'Oh, I don't know!' she said. 'I don't know where he is. I don't know if he *is* my husband!'

'But you have a friend,' Alec said. 'Me. And I've decided that you must be comfortable. I've given some money to your parents.'

'Oh, Alec! I cannot take any gifts from you,' said Tess. 'It's not right.'

'It *is* right,' he said, and he walked away.

Tess tried to work after this, but she could not. Her tears fell onto the soft ground. After a few minutes, she stopped working and began to walk back to the house. Suddenly, she saw Hope, one of her sisters, running towards her.

'Oh, Tess!' the girl cried. 'Mother is much better, but father is dead!'

——

The news was bad, but there was worse news to come. Jack Durbeyfield was dead and the farmer who owned the family's cottage wanted it for his other workers. So the Durbeyfields had to leave their home. Tess thought that this trouble was her fault. The people of Marlott did not like her.

'They remember that I had a child before I got married,' she said to herself. 'I was wrong to come here. The villagers don't want me here, so mother and the children have to leave!'

Tess was angry. She was angry with herself, and she was angry with Angel Clare.

'He's been cruel to me!' she thought. 'Why did he punish me? I didn't *mean* to do wrong!'

That night, Tess wrote an angry letter to Angel.

Oh, why did you punish me, Angel? I have thought about those days after our wedding again and again. You treated me badly. I can never forgive you! You are very cruel! Now I will try to forget you!

Tess

She took the letter to the post office and then came back to the cottage. She sat down by the window in the kitchen. Some minutes later, Alec d'Urberville rode along the street by the house. He saw Tess sitting by the window. He turned the horse around and came up to the wall of the cottage. He knocked on the window and she opened it to speak with him.

'I've heard that you're going away,' said Alec. 'Where are you going?'

'To Kingsbere,' said Tess. 'My mother has found lodgings[83] for us there. We are leaving on 6th April.'

'Listen, I want to help you,' said Alec. 'Come and stay at Trantridge. Your mother can live comfortably in the cottage on the farm, and I'll send the children to a good school.'

'No,' said Tess. 'No, I cannot live at Trantridge.'

'Please tell your mother,' he said. 'I'll ask a servant to clean the house. You can come there immediately. I'll expect to see you tomorrow.'

'No!' said Tess. 'I will not come! I – I can get money!'

'Where? How?' asked Alec.

'From – from the father of my husband!' said Tess.

'But you won't ask him for money,' Alec said angrily. 'I know you, Tess!' And he rode away.

Tess stayed by the window until it was dark.

The next day, the Durbeyfields hired a wagon and a driver. They put all their furniture and possessions[84] into the wagon and went to Kingsbere. At midday, the driver of the wagon stopped at an inn to rest the horse and to get a drink. At the inn, Tess saw Marian and Izz. The two girls had left Flintcomb-Ash because the work was too hard.

'That man came to see you,' Marian told Tess.

'Which man?' asked Tess.

'The gentleman who was once a preacher,' said Marian. 'He asked about you, but we didn't tell him anything.'

'Well, he followed me and found me at my home,' said Tess.

'Does he know where you're going now?' asked Izz.

'Yes,' said Tess.

'Has your husband returned from Brazil?' asked Marian.

'No,' said Tess.

Soon after this conversation, Izz and Marian left the inn and the Durbeyfields continued their journey. It was late when Tess and her family arrived at Kingsbere. At the edge of the town, a man came towards them.

'Are you Mrs Durbeyfield, the widow of Jack Durbeyfield?' the man asked Tess's mother.

'Yes,' said Mrs Durbeyfield. 'But my husband was the noble Sir John d'Urberville.'

'Oh?' said the man. 'Well, I don't know anything about that. But the lodgings that you wanted are full. We only received your letter this morning, and then it was too late. Other people have moved into the rooms.'

'Oh, what can we do now, Tess?' cried Mrs Durbeyfield.

The family went on into the town. Tess stayed with the wagon and the younger children, while her mother and Liza-Lu went to look for other lodgings in Kingsbere. They returned to the wagon after an hour.

'There are no other rooms for us,' said Tess's mother. 'Everywhere is full.'

The wagon driver had to return to Marlott that night. So the Durbeyfields took all their things off the wagon and put them against the wall of the church. The graves of many noble d'Urbervilles were under the ground inside Kingsbere Church. There was also a beautiful window in the church that had pictures of d'Urberville knights on it. But the noble Durbeyfields had nowhere to live. All their furniture and possessions were lying in the street outside the church of Kingsbere.

Mrs Durbeyfield took Liza-Lu and Abraham into the town to buy some food. Hope, Modesty and the younger boys got into the bed and fell asleep. Tess went into the church.

When Mrs Durbeyfield got to the centre of the town, she saw a man looking about him as he rode his horse along the street. It was Alec d'Urberville.

'I was looking for you,' he said to Mrs Durbeyfield. 'Where is Tess?'

'She's at the church,' said Joan Durbeyfield. She did not like Alec d'Urberville, and she walked on quickly.

Alec went to the church and opened the door quietly. Tess was inside, looking up at the great window. She did not see him enter.

Alec walked quietly to a large stone which covered the grave of a d'Urberville. He lay on the gravestone and watched Tess. When she turned and saw him lying on the cold stone, she was shocked.

'Oh!' said Tess, putting her hand on her heart. 'You – you frightened me. What do *you* want?'

He lay on the gravestone and watched Tess.

Alec smiled and looked up at the d'Urberville window. Then he looked at the names written on the d'Urberville gravestones.

'*I* can be more useful to you than a *real* d'Urberville,' he said. 'The real d'Urbervilles are in their graves. I'm here. How can I help you? Tell me.'

'Go away!' said Tess.

'All right, I will,' Alec said. He jumped down from the stone. As he walked past Tess, he whispered to her. 'I'll go and find your mother,' he said. 'You'll soon thank me!' And he went away.

———

After meeting the Durbeyfields at the inn, Marian and Izz continued their journey. They talked about Tess and Alec d'Urberville.

'He follows Tess and watches her,' said Izz. 'He wants her to go with him. But what can we do?'

'Perhaps we could write to Angel Clare,' said Marian. 'We can tell him about the troubles that Tess and her family have. We can tell him about the d'Urberville man.'

'Yes,' said Izz. 'Then perhaps Mr Clare will come home and look after Tess.'

The two women thought about this for the rest of their journey. After that, they were busy moving into their new lodgings. They did not have time to think about Tess and Alec d'Urberville. But a month later, they heard that Angel Clare was coming home, so they wrote to him. They sent the letter to his parents' house in Emminster.

Dear Sir,

If you love your wife as much as she loves you, hurry home. Find her. She is in danger. Someone is pretending to be a friend. He wants her to go away with him. She cannot be strong forever.

From Two Good Friends

11

'Blood! It's Blood!'

It was evening at the Clares' house in Emminster. Reverend and Mrs Clare were sitting by the fire. They were waiting for their son.

'Angel's train reaches Chalk-Newton at six o'clock,' said Reverend Clare. 'Then he must ride ten miles on our old horse to get here.'

The time passed and it became dark. At last the two old people heard a noise outside. They hurried to the front door and opened it. Angel Clare was standing in the shadows.

'Oh, my boy!' said Mrs Clare. 'You are home again at last!'

Angel stepped inside the house and the light from the fire shone on his face. His parents were shocked. He had changed.

'Angel! You are not the same son who went away!' Mrs Clare cried.

His father looked sadly at the thin, tired man in front of him. Angel looked twenty years older.

'I have been ill,' said Angel. 'I'm all right now.'

But he was so tired that he nearly fell into the chair when he sat down.

'Has any letter come for me?' he asked.

They gave him the last letter from Tess. It began with the words: Oh, *why did you punish me, Angel?*

'Everything that she says is true!' said Angel, after he had finished reading. 'I was cruel! Perhaps she will never forgive me.'

'Angel, don't be upset,' said his mother. 'She is only a simple country girl,'

'A simple country girl?' repeated Angel. 'Let me explain something to you. I never told you before, but Tess comes from a noble family. She is a member of the oldest, most noble family in the country.'

The next morning, Angel wrote a letter to Tess and sent it to Marlott. Three days later, a reply came from Mrs Durbeyfield. But her letter had not been written in Marlott.

Sir,

My daughter is not with me. I will write and tell you when she returns. I cannot tell you where she is staying. My family and I are not living at Marlott now.

Joan Durbeyfield

Angel rested and waited for more news about Tess. He became stronger each day.

Then one day he read again the first letter from Tess. It had been sent to him in Brazil. Angel read the words: *But please be kind and come to me now! I'll be happy if I can die in your arms.* His eyes filled with tears. He knew that he had to find Tess immediately. As he was getting ready to leave Emminster, the letter from Izz and Marian arrived. When he read this letter which was from *Two Good Friends*, he left the house quickly.

First, Angel went to Flintcomb-Ash, but could not find Tess there. People remembered Tess by her first name. But they did not know that she was 'Mrs Clare'. Angel was sad when he heard this. He saw where Tess had worked. He realized how hard Tess's life had been. She had refused to ask his father for money, so she had worked in the fields for many hours.

Next, Angel went to Marlott. But the people living in the Durbeyfields' cottage knew nothing about Tess. When he went through the churchyard in Marlott, he saw a new gravestone with John Durbeyfield's name on it. A villager saw him looking at the grave.

'Jack Durbeyfield didn't want to be buried here, sir,' the man said. 'He wanted to be buried in Kingsbere with the rest of the d'Urbervilles. But he had no money to pay for a grave there. And this gravestone isn't paid for yet.'

Angel paid for the gravestone, and heard that the Durbeyfields were now living in the village of Shaston. He went to Shaston and found that Mrs Durbeyfield and her children were living in a house on the edge of the village. He knocked on the door and Joan Durbeyfield opened it. This was the first time that Angel had met Mrs Durbeyfield and he explained that he was Tess's husband.

'I want to see Tess,' said Angel. 'You were going to write to me again, but you didn't.'

'I didn't write again because Tess hasn't come home,' said Mrs Durbeyfield.

'Is she well?' asked Angel.

'I don't know. *You* should know if she is well,' said Mrs Durbeyfield. '*You* should know where she is living. She's your wife!'

'You are right, I *should* know this,' said Angel. 'Where is she staying?'

Mrs Durbeyfield turned her head away from him. 'I – I don't know.' She did not want to tell this stranger where her daughter was living.

'Does she want me to find her?' he asked.

'No,' said Mrs Durbeyfield.

'I'm sure that she does,' he said. 'I know your daughter's feelings better than you. Please tell me her address, Mrs Durbeyfield. Please be kind to a lonely, unhappy man!'

After a moment, Mrs Durbeyfield spoke again.

'She's at Sandbourne,' she said. 'That's all I know.'

'Thank you,' said Angel. 'Do you and your family need anything? Do you need money?'

'No, sir,' she said. 'We're all right.'

Angel turned and walked away. He went to the railway station and got on the next train to Sandbourne.

———

Angel took a room at one of the hotels in Sandbourne. Then he sent a telegram[85] to his father. He told him where he was staying.

After this, he went for a walk in the streets because he could not sleep. Sandbourne was a pleasant town beside the sea. It had parks and large fashionable houses. Where could Tess be in a place like this? There were no cows to milk here. There were no fields to work in.

'Perhaps she is working in one of the large houses,' Angel thought.

At midnight, he returned to his hotel and went to bed.

In the morning, Angel got up early and went out. As he got to the post office, a postman was coming out of the door.

'Do you know the address of a lady named Mrs Clare, or Miss Durbeyfield?' Angel asked him.

'No, but there's a person named d'Urberville at a lodgings called The Herons,' said the postman.

'That's her!' said Angel. 'How do I get to The Herons?'

The postman told him.

The owner of The Herons lodgings was Mrs Brooks. She opened the front door when Angel knocked on it. He asked to see Tess Durbeyfield, or Tess d'Urberville.

'Mrs d'Urberville is staying here,' said the woman. 'What is your name, sir?'

'Angel,' he said.

'Mr Angel?'

'No, just Angel. Tell her that Angel wants to see her. She'll understand.'

He waited in a room downstairs while Mrs Brooks went upstairs.

'It's too late!' Tess said. 'Don't come close to me, Angel!'

'What will Tess think of me?' Angel thought. 'I look so different now.'

When Tess came into the room, Angel got a shock. Tess was wearing expensive clothes and she looked very beautiful. She looked more beautiful than he had remembered. He held out his arms to her, but they fell to his sides again when she did not move.

'Tess!' he cried. 'Can you forgive me for going away? Please ... let me hold you!'

'It's too late!' Tess said, in a cold, hard voice. 'Don't come close to me, Angel! Stay away!'

'I've been ill,' he said. 'That is why I didn't come to you earlier. But now I've come to find you. My mother and father know everything, and they'll welcome you.'

'It's too late,' Tess said again. 'I waited and waited for you. I wrote to you, but you didn't come. He said that you'd never come back again. He was very kind to me and to my family after my father died, and —'

'He?' said Angel. 'I don't understand.'

'He's – he's got me now,' said Tess.

Angel looked at her and understood. He realized that she was speaking about Alec d'Urberville. D'Urberville! The man who had destroyed his happiness.

'He's upstairs,' Tess went on. 'I hate him, because he told me a lie. He said that you wouldn't come back, but you have! But please go away, Angel! Don't come again.'

Angel and Tess looked at each other. They were both sad and confused[86].

'This is my fault, Tess,' Angel said at last. 'It's my fault that —' But he could not go on.

After a few moments, he realized that Tess had left the room. And so he left the house and went out into the street.

Mrs Brooks heard Angel Clare leave her lodgings. She usually cared more about the money that her lodgers paid her than the lodgers themselves. But Mrs d'Urberville and her thin, sad visitor were interesting. Mrs Brooks had heard some of their conversation, but not all of it. When Tess went upstairs to her rooms, Mrs Brooks followed her quietly and listened outside the door.

At first, Mrs Brooks could only hear the sound, 'O–o–o–oh! O–o–o–oh!' coming from the room. She looked through the keyhole of the door and saw Tess sitting on the floor. She was leaning on a chair and her hands were on her head.

Then Mrs Brooks heard a man's voice come from the next room. 'What's the matter?' said the voice.

'My dear, dear husband has come home to me!' cried Tess. 'You said, "He'll never come back", and I believed you. But he did come back! Angel came back to me. Now he's gone away, and I've lost him for ever. He won't love me any more, he'll hate me.'

Then Tess lifted her head and Mrs Brooks could see the pain on Tess's face. Tears were falling from her eyes.

'And Angel is very ill. He's dying!' Tess cried. 'My shame will kill *him*, and not me. Oh, you ruined my life, Alec, and now you have destroyed me! Oh, I cannot live like this!'

Mrs Brooks heard some angry words from the man. Then she heard Tess getting up quickly from the floor. When she heard this, Mrs Brooks hurried back down the stairs.

Mrs Brooks finished her breakfast, and listened to the sound of someone walking above her, in the d'Urbervilles' rooms. The footsteps walked across the rooms and back again, many times. A few minutes later, she saw Tess leaving the house.

Mrs Brooks waited. By this time in the morning, Mr d'Urberville usually asked her to collect the breakfast things[87]. But Mrs Brooks heard nothing. She looked up at the white ceiling above her – and suddenly saw a red spot in the middle. Slowly, the spot got bigger … and bigger.

101

'The gentleman is dead! There's a knife in his chest and a lot of
blood on the floor!'

'Blood!' she cried. 'It's blood!'

She ran up the stairs. DRIP ... DRIP ... DRIP ... was the only sound that she heard. It was coming from the d'Urbervilles' rooms.

Mrs Brooks ran down the stairs and out into the street. A neighbour[88] was walking past and she called to him. She told him what she had seen and heard. They ran up to the d'Urbervilles' rooms together, and Mrs Brooks opened the door.

The breakfast things were still on the table. But a large knife was missing. The neighbour went into the bedroom. He came out again seconds later, his face was white with shock.

'The gentleman is dead!' he said. 'There's a knife in his chest and a lot of blood on the floor!'

Forty minutes later, The Herons was full of police officers. And everyone in Sandbourne was talking about the news. Mrs Brooks' lodger had been killed with a knife!

12

Peace at Last

Angel Clare returned to his hotel. He sat in the dining-room and ate his breakfast. He stared at the walls and ate and drank without thinking. After this, he paid for his room and got ready to leave.

Suddenly, a telegram arrived from his mother. Her telegram gave him the news that his brother, Cuthbert, was going to marry Mercy Chant. Angel read the telegram, then threw the piece of paper away.

Angel Clare picked up his bag and walked to the railway station. There was no train to Emminster for an hour or more, so he sat down to wait. But after fifteen minutes he stood up again. He was restless – he could not sit still. He wanted to get out of Sandbourne quickly.

Angel started walking to the station in the next town.

'I can get the train there,' he thought.

The road went out of the town, then down across a valley. Angel was climbing the hill on the western side of the valley when he stopped to rest. Suddenly he turned and looked round. Someone was running after him. It was a woman.

Angel waited. He did not recognize Tess, until she was very near to him.

'I saw you ... turn away from the station ... just before I got there!' she said, breathing quickly. 'I've followed you all this way!'

Tess's face was pale and she was shaking. Angel did not ask any questions. He just held her hand and helped her along the road. They went down a path through some trees. They would not meet anybody on this lonely narrow path. Angel stopped and Tess turned towards him.

'Angel,' she said. She was smiling sadly. 'I've killed him.'

'What!' said Angel.

He saw her strange smile, and thought, 'Is she mad?'

'I don't know how I did it,' Tess continued. 'I've killed Alec d'Urberville. I had to do it. I did it for you and for myself. I never loved him, Angel. Do you believe me? Alec brought shame on my family. He ruined me and destroyed our lives – yours and mine. It wasn't your fault. But he can't hurt us any more. Oh, why did you go away? I loved you so much. Oh, I feel no anger towards you. But will you forgive me, now that I've killed him? Say that you love me, my dear, dear husband!'

'I do love you, Tess, oh I do!' Angel said, and he put his arms around her. 'But I don't understand. Have you really killed d'Urberville? Is he really dead?'

'Yes,' she said. 'Alec heard me crying and calling your

104

name. He said cruel things. Then he called you a bad name, and – and I did it! I killed him. Then I came to find you.'

Slowly, Angel began to believe Tess. She probably *had* killed Alec d'Urberville. Or she had *tried* to kill him.

'My darling Tess's love for me is so strong,' Angel thought. 'It makes her forget the difference between right and wrong. Does she understand what she's done? I don't think that she does.'

It was a terrible story, if it was true. But Angel had to look after Tess. He could not leave her now. He kissed her again and again. He felt only love for her.

'I won't leave you, Tess, my dearest love!' said Angel.

Tess put her head on Angel's shoulder and cried with happiness.

They walked on through the trees. Every few minutes, Tess turned to look at Angel. She did not see the tired, thin man that he was now. She saw only the handsome young man that she had seen at the May Dance in Marlott. The man that she had fallen in love with at Talbothays Dairy.

Angel did not go towards the railway station in the next town. Instead, he took her further into the woods.

After several miles, Tess asked, 'Where are we going?'

'I don't know,' said Angel. 'Perhaps we will find some lodgings this evening. Can you walk a few more miles, Tess?'

'Oh, yes,' she said. 'Your arm is around me, dearest Angel. I could walk for ever.'

They travelled on quiet lonely paths. But they did not try to hide from anyone. At midday, they stopped near an inn. Angel told Tess to wait in a wood. He went to the inn to buy some food and two bottles of wine. They sat down under a tree and shared their meal, then they walked on again.

'I think that we should go north, towards London,' said Angel. 'From there we can get on a ship and go to another country. Ships go to every part of the world from London.'

Tess and Angel walked on through the warm afternoon, but by the evening they needed somewhere to rest.

'Could we sleep in a wood?' asked Tess.

'No. It is May but it is cold at night,' Angel said.

Then they came to a large house which was surrounded by many trees.

'I know this place,' said Angel. 'It's called Bramshurst House. It is empty and locked up until the summer.'

'Some of the windows are open,' said Tess. 'Perhaps they are open so some air goes into the rooms. Oh, here is an empty house, and we don't have a place to sleep!'

'Wait here, under the trees, Tess,' said Angel. Then he walked towards the house.

After quite a long time, he returned.

'I spoke to a young boy,' he said to Tess. 'He told me that nobody is living in the house just now. An old woman comes to clean the rooms. She opens and shuts some of the windows on fine days. She'll come and shut the window tonight. I think that we can rest safely in this house.'

Tess and Angel got into the house through a window beside the front door. Then they went up the stairs, to one of the bedrooms. There was a large bed in the middle of the room.

'We can rest here at last!' said Angel, putting down his bag.

At six-thirty that evening, the old woman came to shut the windows. Tess and Angel sat quietly and listened until she went away again. Then they ate the rest of their food before lying on the bed.

The night was strangely quiet. There were no sounds from the birds or animals who lived in the wood surrounding the house.

The next morning, the weather was wet and foggy. Angel woke first and for a long time he watched Tess sleeping.

'It's wet and cool outside,' he thought. 'The old woman won't open the windows today.'

He got up from the bed and looked through the other rooms in the house for some food. He could not find any. Then he went outside. The thick fog almost hid the trees that surrounded the house.

Angel walked to a shop in the little town, two miles away. He bought some bread, butter and tea, and returned to Bramshurst House.

When Angel returned, Tess woke up and they ate their breakfast.

———

Tess and Angel stayed in the house for the next five days. They saw nobody, and they heard only the birds in the wood. They watched the changing weather. Sometimes the sun shone, but most of the time cold rain fell from large, grey clouds.

Angel and Tess did not speak at all about the sad, difficult days since their wedding. Several times, Angel suggested that they went on to Southampton or London. But Tess did not want to leave Bramshurst House.

'Why should we end our happy life together?' she said. 'What must happen, will happen.' She looked out of the window. 'Outside there is only trouble. Here, inside, there is peace.'

Angel went and looked out of the window, too. It was true. The house was a safe place of love and forgiveness. The world outside was where cruel and painful things happened.

'And,' Tess went on, 'I'm afraid that you'll stop loving me one day. I'm afraid that the loving feelings that you have now will disappear. Angel, I want to die before you begin to hate me.'

'I'll never hate you,' he said.

'I hope that is true,' said Tess. 'I remember my past life and

Sunlight came through the window and shone on the two beautiful, innocent faces of Angel and Tess.

I understand why any man would hate me. I was very wicked! I murdered Alec! I must have been mad when I killed him!'

———

They stayed in the house another day. During the night, the clouds disappeared from the sky. The next morning, the sun shone.

The old woman decided to open all of the windows in the house that day. She came before six o'clock, while Tess and Angel were still sleeping. After opening the windows of the rooms downstairs, she walked up the stairs to the bedrooms. And in one of the bedrooms she found the lovers.

At first, the woman was shocked and angry. But sunlight came through the window and shone on the two beautiful, innocent faces of Angel and Tess. And her anger disappeared.

The old woman did not wake the lovers, but hurried out of the house, to tell her neighbours.

A minute after she went away, Tess and Angel woke up. They both felt that someone or something in the house had woken them. And they both felt that they were no longer safe in the house.

'We must leave immediately,' Angel said.

They got dressed, collected their things, and left. When they had gone a little way along the road, Tess looked back at the house.

'Oh, happy house – goodbye!' she said. 'I will not live more than a few more weeks. I'm sure about this.'

'Don't say that, Tess!' said Angel. 'We'll get to a ship in two or three days and we'll go overseas. But perhaps we should not go to London or Southampton. We could get on a ship at Bristol. No one will look for us there.'

By the middle of the day, they had reached the edge of the city of Melchester. Angel bought some more food and they rested under some trees. When it was dark, the lovers started walking again.

At three o'clock in the morning, Tess and Angel found a road that took them across open land. As they started to walk along this road, the moon went behind the clouds. The night became as black as ink. Tess and Angel walked on the soft grass beside the road and their footsteps made no sound. After two or three miles, Angel saw the shape of a big stone against the dark sky. The stone was taller than two or three men – and it came straight up out of the grass. Angel and Tess had nearly walked into it.

'What terrible place is this?' said Angel.

'Listen,' said Tess.

The wind blew around the huge stone and made strange, musical sounds. Suddenly the clouds moved across the sky and moonlight shone down. Tess and Angel now saw that there were more stones around them. Several of the pairs of tall stones had a third enormous stone lying across the tops of them. Tess and Angel walked carefully beneath and between them. They were in the middle of a ring of stones now.

'This is Stonehenge!' said Angel. 'This is an old temple[89]! The first people of Britain built this ring of stones. They came here to pray to their gods. Stonehenge is thousands of years old. It's older than the d'Urbervilles!'

Tess was very tired. She lay down on one of the flat stones. It was warm and dry.

'I don't want to go further, Angel,' she said. 'Can we stay here?'

'No, dearest, we can't,' he said. 'We're not safe here. In the daylight, you can see this place from miles around.'

'I like it here,' said Tess. 'It's quiet and lonely. Here, only the sky is above my face. I can pretend that we are the only people in the world. Oh, I wish that there *weren't* any other people – except Liza-Lu! If anything happens to me, Angel, will you look after Liza-Lu?'

'I will,' he said.

110

Angel put his coat over Tess, and sat down next to her on the stone.

'Liza-Lu is good and simple and innocent,' said Tess. 'Oh, Angel! I will be gone soon! Then you must marry her.'

'If you go, I will have lost everything that is good,' he said.

'Liza-Lu is innocent and honest, as I once was,' said Tess. 'If you and she are together, I will be happy. I will feel that death had not pulled us apart.'

Then they were both silent. Each of them looked at the sky and thought about Tess's words. Now Angel could see the first light of the day shining down between the clouds.

'Tell me, dear,' Tess said suddenly. 'Do you think that we'll meet again after we're dead?'

Angel kissed her but he did not answer.

'Oh Angel, that means no!' she cried. 'You *don't* think that we'll meet after our deaths! And I wanted to see you again – more than anything! Are you sure that we will never be together again? We love each other so much!'

Angel could not answer her, and they were silent again. After a minute or two Tess fell asleep.

As time passed, the wind became quiet and the sky became lighter. It was almost dawn. Suddenly Angel saw someone far in the distance. It was a man, and he was coming towards them.

Angel wished that they had gone to Bristol, but it was too late now. He did not say anything, or wake Tess.

Then he heard a sound behind him. He turned and saw another man, then another and another. Police officers were walking towards the ring of great stones. So Tess's story was true! She *had* killed Alec d'Urberville!

Angel jumped up and looked around for a way to escape.

'You can't get away, sir,' said the nearest police officer. 'There are sixteen of us here, and there are other officers waiting a little further away.'

'What is it, Angel? Have they come for me?'

'Please, let her sleep a little longer!' Angel whispered. And the men came to stand around the stone where Tess was sleeping.

Angel held Tess's hand. The men waited as the daylight became brighter. Soon the sun shone on Tess's face and she woke.

'What is it, Angel?' she said, and sat up. 'Have they come for me?'

'Yes, dearest,' he said. 'They've come.'

'It's only right,' said Tess. 'Angel, I'm almost glad. This happiness could not have gone on. And now I won't live long enough for you to hate me.'

She got off the stone and went towards the police officers.

'I am ready,' she said quietly.

———

On a warm morning in July, the sun shone down on the fine old city of Wintoncester.

It was the beginning of a busy market day. Two people were walking quickly up the hill which rose up to the west of the city. The man and the young woman walked silently, with their heads down. The man was Angel Clare and the young woman was Tess's younger sister, Liza-Lu. Angel was holding Liza-Lu's hand.

When they were near the top of the great West Hill, the bells in the city's clocks rang eight times. Eight o'clock. The young people stopped and turned round to look sadly at the city below them. They could see the tall buildings of Wintoncester Cathedral[90] and the college. And they could see the prison.

The prison was a large building made of red bricks and it had a grey roof. Below the roof were rows of small windows with iron bars across them. A tall post was fixed to the roof of the prison.

A few minutes after eight o'clock, something moved very

slowly up the post. It was a black flag. Whenever a prisoner was hanged[91], a black flag flew from the roof of the prison.

When they saw the flag, Angel and Liza-Lu knew that Tess was dead. She was at peace at last.

Liza-Lu and Angel dropped down onto their knees and prayed to God. Then they got up slowly, and holding each other's hands, walked on.

Points for Understanding

1

1 Who is the drunken man?
2 What news does he hear and who tells him this news?
3 Which custom is being celebrated in the village?
4 Who watches the celebration?
5 What bad luck happens the next day?

2

1 Two families call themselves d'Urberville. But who are the *real* descendents of the old and noble d'Urberville family, and why?
2 Which people are connected to these words? (a) smiling, gifts, strawberries (b) beautiful, innocent, blushing (c) blind, widow, chickens

3

'Since Tess last saw her home, her life had changed.' How has Tess's life changed?

4

1 Why does Tess go to Talbothays and what does she do there?
2 'For a moment, she was worried. Did the man recognize her?'
   (a) Who has Tess met?
   (b) What does she think about this person?
   (c) What does this person think about her?

5

1 Who is in love with whom?
2 What kind of woman does Reverend Clare think will be the best wife for Angel?

3 ' "But I've met someone else." ' Why does Angel think that this person will be a better wife than Mercy Chant?
4 ' "But I can never marry you!" ' Who says this and why?

6

1 Tess agrees to marry Angel. Then, on the journey from the railway station to Talbothays, she tells him something about her past life.
  (a) What does she tell him?
  (b) What does she not tell him?
2 What happens on Christmas Eve?
3 What happens in the morning on 31st December?
4 A wedding should be a happy celebration. But Tess and Angel's marriage does not start well. What things happen which show this?

7

1 On their wedding night, Angel and Tess tell each other about their mistakes.
  (a) What was Angel's mistake?
  (b) What was Tess's mistake?
2 Why cannot Angel truly forgive Tess?
3 What happens on 4th January?
4 'Nobody could love you more than Tess. She would die for you.'
  (a) Who says these words to Angel?
  (b) Why did this person say these words?

8

1 Tess leaves Marlott. (a) Who does she meet on the road?
  (b) Where does she go? (c) Who does she work with?
  (d) Who is she working for?
2 Why does Tess go to Emminster and what happens when she gets there?

9

1 Who is the 'changed man'?
2 How has this person changed?
3 ' "If you are *any* man's wife, you are *mine!*" ' Who says this? Why?

10

1 Tess writes to Angel and asks for his help. She thinks that
   something terrible is going to happen to her. Who or what is she
   afraid of?
2 Why does Liza-Lu come to Flintcomb-Ash?
3 (a) Who watches Tess as she works in the allotment? (b) What
   does this person say that he is going to do?
4 Which two bad things happen to the Durbeyfield family after this?
5 Tess writes a second letter to Angel. How does she feel about him
   now?
6 Why is the church at Kingsbere important for the Durbeyfields?
7 Who has written a letter to Angel giving him a warning?

11

Mrs Brooks runs up the stairs of her lodgings at Sandbourne. Why?

12

When Angel and Tess arrive at Stonehenge, the night is described
as 'black as ink'. Then ' ... suddenly the clouds moved and
moonlight shone down from the sky' and the lovers see the
strange and mysterious place for the first time. Hardy uses
descriptions of the weather and the countryside in this novel to
show the feelings of the characters. These descriptions also warn
the reader that something is going to happen to the characters.
Look back. Find three examples of descriptions used in this way.

Glossary

At the time of this story, British measurements were in *miles, yards, feet* and *inches*. 1 inch = 25.3995 mm, 1 foot = 30.479 cm, 1 yard = 0.9144 m, 1 mile = 1.6093 km.

1   **county** (page 4)
    the United Kingdom of Great Britain is made up of England, Scotland, Wales and Northern Ireland. Each of these areas are divided into smaller areas called *counties*. Hardy wrote about an area which he called Wessex. (See the map on page 10.) He also used different names for the villages, towns and cities in this area.

2   **quarrels** (page 5)
    arguments between people who know each other well.

3   **guilty** – *to feel guilty* (page 6)
    Hardy felt sorry because of the unkind things that he had said to Emma when she was alive.

4   **country** (page 6)
    the land outside towns, where there are farms, trees, mountains and lakes, is called the *countryside*. This word is often shortened to *country*.

5   **celebrate** – *to celebrate* (page 6)
    when people want to remember a special time or event, they meet together to enjoy themselves. For example, the people of Marlott *celebrate* the beginning of spring – the time of year when all things begin to grow again. The women of the village sing songs and dance. The villagers' *celebration* is called the May Walk and Dance because they are celebrating it in the month of May. (See Glossary 21.)

6   **hired** – *to hire* (page 7)
    pay a person to do some work for you. If you *hire something* from someone, you pay to use the thing that they own.

7   **cereal crops** (page 7)
    plants which are grown so that their seeds – the *grain* – can be made into food. Examples of *cereal crops* are oats, rye and maize. Examples of *vegetable crops* are potatoes, cabbages and turnips.

8   **hedges** (page 7)
    lines of trees and bushes which grow around the sides of fields. *Hedges* stop animals from leaving their fields.

118

9   **harvested** – *to harvest* (page 7)
    when crops have finished growing and are ready to eat, they are *harvested*. The farm workers who do this work are called *harvesters*. At the time of this story, machines were starting to do some of the work on farms. Two of these new machines were the *harvesting machine* and the *threshing machine*.
    The *harvesting machine* was pulled by strong horses. It cut the stalks of the cereal plants. Then the stalks were tied together in *bundles* by the farm workers. The bundles were left in the sun to become dry. These bundles were kept together during the winter in a big pile called a *rick*.
    Later the bundles were put in a *threshing machine*. This machine was powered by a steam engine. The threshing machine removed the dry grains from the stalks of the plant.
    When vegetables were harvested, farm workers dug them out of the ground.

10 **mills** (page 7)
    buildings where grain is crushed between huge stones. After the grain is crushed, or *ground*, it becomes flour. Flour is used to make bread. At the time of this story, *mills* got their power from the air (windmills) or water (watermills).

11 **allotments** (page 7)
    small areas of land in towns or villages where people can grow their own vegetables or fruit are called *allotments*.

12 **inn** (page 13)
    a place where people can buy alcohol and food, and pay for a bed to sleep in. A *landlord* is a person who owns an inn.

13 **parson** (page 13)
    a Christian priest who travelled around country areas, and held religious meetings, was called a *parson*, or a *preacher*. Parsons *preached* to people – they told them about the Bible and God, and about Heaven and hell. They told people how to *pray* to God and how to behave.
    Christian priests who lived and worked in large churches in towns used the title *Reverend* in front of their names. Christian priests wanted to *save* people – make sure that they did not do bad things or think bad thoughts.

14 **Sir John** (page 13)

a *knight* was an important soldier who fought for a king or queen hundreds of years ago.

NOTE: knight is pronounced **night**. Knights were often powerful members of the king or queen's family. A knight was paid with land and money. He was called by the title *Sir*. For example, Sir John d'Urberville. The title is a *knighthood*.

15 **descendant** (page 13)

relatives are members of a family who do not live together. Your *ancestors* are members of your family who lived many years ago. For example, your father, grandfather, great-grandfather, great-great-grandfather, etc, are your ancestors. You are their *descendant*.

16 **old and noble** (page 13)

an *old and noble* family is a rich, important and powerful family which has existed for very many years.

17 **portraits** (page 14)

paintings of people, showing their faces.

18 **manor houses** (page 14)

large houses in the country which are homes of rich people who own a lot of land.

19 **churchyard** (page 14)

the area around a church where the bodies of dead people are *buried* – put in the ground – is called a *graveyard*. Each dead person is buried in a *grave*. A *gravestone* is put over a grave. The gravestone has the name of the dead person and the dates of their birth and death written on it.

20 **carriage** (page 15)

a *carriage* was a vehicle which had four wheels and was pulled by a horse. The driver sat on a seat in front of the passenger.

A *van* was a vehicle with four wheels that was pulled by one or two horses. Vans had a covering over them. They were used to carry all kinds of goods from one place to another.

A *gig* was a vehicle with two large wheels which was pulled by a fast horse. The passenger sat beside the driver.

A *cart* was a wooden vehicle with two wheels which was pulled by a strong horse.

A *wagon* was a heavy wooden vehicle with four wheels which was pulled by two or more strong horses. Wagons were used on farms and country roads to carry heavy loads.

21 **May Walk and Dance** (page 15)

In Wessex, during the month of May, young girls walked together through their villages. They wore white dresses and they carried branches of green leaves and white flowers. Then they danced and sang songs. This ceremony was called the *May Walk and Dance*.

22 **Vale of Blackmoor** (page 15)

vale is the short form of the word, *valley*. A valley is an area of land that is lower than the ground on both its sides. There is often a river in the bottom of a valley. (See the map on page 10.)

23 **ribbon** (page 16)

the girl has tied a long, thin piece of coloured material in her hair. The *ribbon* holds her hair away from her face and it is also used as a decoration.

24 **in no hurry** (page 16)

the young man does not want to leave the field immediately. He wants to stay and watch the girls dancing. He is *in no hurry*.
When someone *hurries into marriage*, they get married quickly and without thinking.
Someone who is travelling home quickly is *hurrying home*.

25 **common** (page 18)

someone who has had little education, and speaks and behaves in a loud way is *common*. The word is used in an impolite way.

26 **dancing-partners** (page 18)

men and women who dance together.

27 **seemed annoyed** – *to seem to be annoyed* (page 18)

a person who looks upset and angry about something *seems to be annoyed* by that thing.

28 **noticed** – *to notice* (page 18)

suddenly see someone or something.

29 **weak** – *to feel weak* (page 19)

Durbeyfield felt ill and unable to walk. He *felt weak*.

30 **lantern** (page 20)

a glass container with a candle inside it. The glass kept the wind away from the candle so that the *lantern* could be carried outside. There was no electricity in country homes at this time so people used candles and lanterns.

31 **specially glad** (page 20)

more pleased than usual.

32 **put that idea in your head** (page 20)
Tess is asking who gave her brother this information and made him think this way.

33 **mail cart** (page 20)
a vehicle which carried peoples' letters and parcels between the towns and villages. A fast horse pulled a *mail cart*.

34 **speeding** (page 20)
the mail cart was moving very fast and dangerously.

35 **It was my fault** (page 22)
when you do something which makes a problem for another person, *it is your fault* that they have a problem.

36 **my beauty** (page 23)
the words that someone says to a person who they like and know well. It is a way that a person talks to a woman if they think she is beautiful. The young man does not know Tess but he is talking to her in a informal and personal way. My *darling* and *my dearest* are the words that a person uses to someone whom they know and love.

37 **blind** (page 28)
unable to see.

38 **healthy** (page 28)
strong and well.

39 **whistle** – *to whistle* (page 28)
make a sound when you blow through your teeth and lips. The sound is *whistling*.

40 **ma'am** (page 28)
a shortened form of *madam* – a polite way of talking to a woman in the nineteenth century.

41 **fog** (page 30)
a thick cloud that comes down close to the ground. When there is *fog*, the weather is *foggy*.

42 **make love** – *to make love to someone* (page 30)
in old English – when someone says and does things which show that they are in love with another person, they are *making love to* that person.
This phrase today has a stronger meaning. *To make love to someone* means that a person has sexual intercourse with someone.

122

43 **bundle** (page 32)

many things are tied together in a *bundle*. For example, clothes can be put into a bundle. See also Glossary 9.

44 **innocent** (page 32)

a good, kind person who has never done anything bad is *innocent*. A young, unmarried girl who has never had sex with a man is an *innocent* girl, or a *maiden*.

45 **wickedness** (page 32)

bad or evil things. Someone who does bad and evil things is *wicked*. Christian girls were taught that they must not have sex with a man who was not their husband.

46 **treated** – *to treat* (page 32)

the way a person talks and behaves towards someone. Tess now believes that all rich gentlemen behave badly towards country girls. They have sex with them and then leave them.

47 **warn** – *to warn someone* (page 36)

tell someone about trouble or danger that might happen in the future.

48 **hymns** (page 36)

songs that Christians sing in a church to praise God. The word is pronounced **him**.

49 **protect** – *to protect* (page 36)

stop something from hurting or injuring someone or something.

50 **bonnet** (page 36)

a hat worn by a woman. Women in the country wore *bonnets* made of cotton or straw. The front and the sides of a bonnet kept the hot sun off a woman's face while she was working. A *veil* was a piece of thin cloth which covered a woman's face.

51 **shocked** – *to be shocked* (page 37)

be surprised and upset by something that you have seen or heard.

52 **baptised** – *to be baptised* (page 37)

a ceremony when a priest welcomes someone into the Christian church. If that person is a child, then the child is given his or her name during this ceremony. Some Christians believe that if a child is *baptised*, they will go to Heaven when they die. They believe that if a person dies before they are baptised, that person will go to hell. And they will have pain and sadness for ever.

53 **refused** – *to refuse* (page 39)

to not do, or allow, something that someone has asked you to do.

123

54 **ruined** – *to be ruined* (page 39)
at the time of this story, if a man had sex with a woman who was not his wife, and later she had a child, she was *ruined*.
The child was her *shame*. The child reminded people of what the woman had done. People thought that these women were bad and dishonest. The woman lost her good name.

55 **milked** – *to be milked* (page 40)
take milk from a cow. Twice each day, the cows came from the fields to the *milking-shed* in the *dairy yard*. The cows came in the morning and in the afternoon. On a *dairy farm* in the 1880s, milk was taken by hand, because there were no machines to do this. The *dairymaids* and *dairymen* sat on *milking stools* – small wooden seats – beside the cows. The milk went into *buckets* – wooden containers. *Churns* were tall metal containers which held the milk. The milk was taken to a cool room – the *dairy-room* – and put in large, square metal containers. Some of the milk was then made into butter, cream and cheese.

56 **green and fertile** (page 40)
the ground is good and there is a lot of water so the plants and grass grow well.

57 **apron** (page 42)
something that you wear over your clothes to keep them clean and dry.

58 **recognize** – *to recognize someone* (page 42)
know who a person is and where you have seen them before.

59 **harp** (page 43)
a musical instrument.

60 **changing seasons** (page 43)
spring, summer, autumn and winter are *seasons*. As the weather gets warmer or colder, drier or wetter, the *seasons change*. The land looks different as the leaves on trees and plants die, or grow again.

61 **spots** (page 43)
small round areas of colour that have been made by a liquid.

62 **puzzled** – *to be puzzled* (page 44)
worry and think about something which is difficult to understand.

63 **wasted my life** – *to waste your life* (page 44)
Tess is saying that she has not lived her life in the best way. She has not done things that are important and she has not used her intelligence well.

64 **shared** – *to share* (page 45)
use or have something at the same time as someone else.
For example, you can *share a room* or *a bed*.
If you *share someone's life*, you are with them in the difficult times
and the good times.

65 **stockings** (page 46)
thin coverings that women wear on their legs.

66 **bend** (page 46)
a place where a road turns to the left or the right.

67 **truly** (page 48)
very much, completely.

68 **pretended** – *to pretend* (page 48)
behave in a way that makes people think that something is true
when it is not.

69 **proposal** (page 53)
when a man asks a woman to marry him, he is making a *proposal of
marriage*.

70 **reins** (page 54)
long pieces of leather which are attached to a horse's mouth. The
reins make the horse go to the right or left.

71 **engaged** – *to be engaged* (page 55)
when a man and a woman agree that they will marry, they *become
engaged*. The time before their marriage is called an *engagement*.

72 **tried to hide her feelings** – *to try to hide your feelings* (page 55)
behave in a special way so that other people will not know what
you think or feel.
Tess makes her face still. She tries to *hide her feelings* of sadness or
happiness.

73 **forgiven** – *to forgive* (page 56)
decide that you will not be angry with someone who has injured
you, or made you upset or unhappy.

74 **tried to drown herself** – *to try to drown yourself* (page 61)
Retty tried to kill herself by staying under the water until she
could no longer breathe.

75 **threw her shadow** – *to throw a shadow* (page 62)
the light from the fire is shining on Tess and a dark *shadow* of her
body has appeared on the wall behind her.

76 **betray** – *to betray* (page 64)
if you *betray* someone's trust, you do harm to them when they have
trusted you.

77 **destroyed his happiness** – *to destroy someone's happiness* (page 64)

do something to someone so that they are never happy again.
Angel had thought that Tess was innocent when he met her. He thought that she had never had sex with a man. Now she has told him about Alec and the baby. He cannot forget this and he is upset and angry. This information has *destroyed his happiness*.

78 **divorce** – *to divorce* (page 64)

when two people want to end their marriage they get a *divorce*. They go to a court and ask for a legal paper which says that their marriage is finished.
Before 1857, people usually had to be married to each other until one of them died. This was the law. At the time of this story, the laws on marriage were being changed. But it was still very difficult for a man and woman *to divorce* each other.

79 **painful memories** (page 79)

thoughts that make someone very sad, or uncomfortable.

80 **junction** (page 79)

a place on the road where two or more roads meet. A traveller can go to the left or to the right, or straight on sometimes.

81 **punished** – *to punish* (page 88)

when someone does something wrong and you hurt them, or make them feel sorry, you are *punishing* them.

82 **trick** – *to trick* (page 85)

make someone believe something that is not true.

83 **lodgings** (page 90)

a place that you pay to live in. If you pay to live in someone's house, you are a *lodger*.

84 **possessions** (page 91)

things that you own.

85 **telegram** (page 98)

at the time of this story there were very few phones. If someone wanted to send an urgent message to a person who was many miles away, they sent a *telegram*. Their message was sent by electronic signals on a *telegraph machine*. *Telegraph operators* looked after the telegraph machines. When an operator received a message, he wrote it on a piece of paper. This paper – the telegram – was then delivered to the person that it was addressed to.

86 **confused** – *to be confused* (page 100)

unable to think clearly about something.

87 **breakfast things** (page 101)
cups, saucers, plates, knives, forks, etc. The things that you use when you eat breakfast.

88 **neighbour** (page 103)
a person who lives near you.

89 **temple** (page 110)
a place where people go to pray to their god, or gods.
The *temple* of Stonehenge was built by British people more than 4000 years ago. It is a large circle of huge, tall stones which stand on high ground near Salisbury in the county of Wiltshire. Some scientists believe that people may have studied the movements of the sun and the moon in the sky at Stonehenge.

90 **Cathedral** (page 113)
a large church where Christians go to pray. *Cathedrals* are built of stone and often have large windows made from pieces of coloured glass.

91 **hanged** – to be hanged (page 114)
at the time of this story, the crime of murder was punished by death. A rope was tied around the murderer's neck and their body was hung until they were dead.

Exercises

What Happened Next?

Number the sentences in the correct order.

	Angel marries Tess.
	Tess works with Angel Clare.
	Tess works for old Mrs d'Urberville.
	Alec d'Urberville becomes a preacher and tries to help Tess.
	Sorrow dies.
	Alec d'Urberville takes Tess to The Chase.
1	Jack Durbeyfield learns that he is a d'Urberville.
	Tess visits Alec d'Urberville and his mother.
	Angel leaves Tess when she tells him she had a child.
	Tess has a child called Sorrow.
	Angel marries Tess's sister Eliza-Louise.
	Tess is arrested and hanged.
	Tess kills Alec d'Urberville.

Grammar Focus 1

Complete the gaps with the past tenses of the verbs.

PRESENT	SIMPLE PAST	PAST PARTICIPLE
visit	*visited*	*visited*
grind		
buy		
bring		
send		
fetch		
grow		

Multiple Choice

Tick the best answer.

Q1 Why didn't Angel's brothers want to dance with the girls at the May Dance?
   a Because they were common country girls. ✓
   b Because they wanted to get home for dinner.
   c Because Angel was laughing at them.
   d Because the girls were laughing at them.

Q2 Why did Tess have to baptise her son herself?
   a Because the parson was sick.
   b Because the baby was too sick to go to the parson.
   c Because her father was ashamed of the parson finding out about her child.
   d Because Tess was ashamed of telling the parson that she has a child.

Q3 Why didn't Tess tell Angel about her "mistake"?
   a Because she was too afraid.
   b Because he asked her to wait until after the wedding.
   c Because she didn't want him to know.
   d Because she didn't think he would care.

Q4 What stopped Angel from sleeping next to Tess on their wedding night?
   a He couldn't sleep.
   b He went back to his parents' house.
   c He saw a portrait of one of Tess's ancestors.
   d Tess was crying.

Q5 What made Alec d'Urberville change his ways?
   a His mother threatened to take all his money away.
   b Angel fought with him.
   c He had nightmares about Tess.
   d He talked to Angel's father, the Reverend James Clare.

Grammar Focus 2: *to be* + past participle

Answer the questions using *to be* and the past participle shown.

Example grind	Why is corn sent to the mill? *Corn is sent to the mill to be ground.*
1 milk	Why are cows brought to the milking shed?
2 make into bread	What is going to be done with the flour?
3 sell	Why are eggs sent to market?
4 corn grow	What is going to be grown in that field?
5 marry	Why did Angel and Tess go to church?
6 arrest	What did Tess expect to happen to her after she killed Alec?
7 harvest	What is going to be done with the corn when it is ripe?
8 give a job	Tess needed some money. What did she want?
9 forgive	Why did Angel try to find Tess?

Words From The Story 1

Complete the sentences with words from the box.

> descendant   common   wicked   treat   refused   ruined
> fertile   ~~guilty~~   whistle   ribbon   harvest   celebrated   noble
> lantern   carriage

1 If you feel .... *guilty* ...., you feel you have done something wrong.

2 The girls in the village .... May Day by singing and dancing.

3 The corn in the fields is ready to cut in August. The time of cutting the corn is called the ....

4 Jack d'Urberville was the great-great grandson of Sir John d'Urberville. Jack Durbeyfield was a .... of Sir John d'Urberville.

5 Sir John d'Urberville was a knight. The d'Urbervilles were an old and .... family.

6 There were no cars or buses in the 1880s. Alec d'Urberville rode in a .... pulled by a horse.

7 Tess tied a piece of red material in her hair. Angel Clare remembered this red .... three years later.

8 This word means *ordinary* or *usual* or *often*, but it also has an unpleasant meaning when applied to people. In the story, ignorant country people are called ....

9 There were no electric lights in the 1880s. People burned candles or oil lamps at night. A kind of lamp with a candle inside is called a ....

10 Mrs d'Urberville wanted Tess to make noises to the chickens. She wanted Tess to .... to the chickens.

11 Another word for very bad or evil (men) is ....

12 Alec d'Urberville was the master of The Slopes and Tess was a servant. Alec behaved badly towards Tess. He did not .... Tess well.

Story Outline

Complete the gaps. Use each word in the box once.

> name carriage mistake angry not walking decided letter
> pushed next kissed read ~~street~~ chin forgiven looked
> writing slept right lovely money nothing make truth
> true speaking said speak moment maiden

As Tess waited in the ¹....*street*.., two men went past. They

²... at her.

'She's a ³... maiden,' the first man

⁴... .

'She's lovely, that is ⁵...,' said the second

man, whose ⁶... was Farmer Groby. 'But

she's not a maiden.'

At that ⁷..., Angel returned and heard the

men ⁸... . Angrily, he jumped from the

⁹... and hit the second man on the

¹⁰... .

'I – I'm sorry, sir,' said Groby. He looked again at Tess. 'I made a

¹¹... .'

After a moment, Angel said, 'All ¹²... .

Perhaps I became ¹³... too quickly. I

should ¹⁴... have hit you.'

Angel gave the man some ¹⁵... then

drove away in the carriage with Tess. The two men continued

¹⁶... along the street.

'Did you ¹⁷... a mistake?' asked the first man.

'No, I didn't,' said Groby. 'She's not a ¹⁸... .'

After this, Tess ¹⁹... to tell Angel the

[20] .... But she did not know how to
[21] .... to him about it. So she decided to
write him a [22] .... When she had finished
[23] .... the letter, she
[24] .... it under the door of Angel's room.
Tess [25] .... badly that night. The
[26] .... morning, Angel came down from his
room and [27] .... her, but he said
[28] .... about the letter. Had he
[29] .... it? Perhaps he had
[30] .... her.

Words From The Story 2

Unjumble the letters to find words from the story. The meanings are given to help you.

Example	DUNBEL
MEANING	a group of things that you tie or wrap together
ANSWER	*bundle*

1	TENINCON
MEANING	you have done nothing wrong, also you do not know the ways of the world
ANSWER	

2	SIGNECORE
MEANING	to know again – someone or something you have seen or heard before
ANSWER	

3	SPOOREP
MEANING	to make a suggestion or to ask someone to marry you
ANSWER	

4	FOCSUNE
MEANING	to mix up ideas or not have a clear understanding or recognition of events
ANSWER	

5	REBAYT
MEANING	do something that harms someone who trusts you
ANSWER	

6	VIDEORC
MEANING	to end a marriage (by law)
ANSWER	

7	TONICJUN
MEANING	a place where roads or railway lines meet
ANSWER	

8	HISPUN
MEANING	make somebody suffer because they have done something wrong
ANSWER	

9	DOGSLING
MEANING	accommodation – such as a room in an inn – where you pay to live or stay
ANSWER	

Making Sentences 1

Rewrite the sentences using a form of the words from the last exercise.

Example	Tess was only sixteen years old and did not understand what Alec wanted.
ANSWER	Tess was young and innocent.

1 Angel did not see Tess again for three years, but he knew her when he saw her.

_____

2 Tess and Angel met at the crossroads.

_____

3 Angel asked Tess to marry him.

_____

4 Tess and Angel were both unhappy and mixed up.

_____

5 Angel left Tess because he said that she had not told him the truth.

_____

6 Tess said that they should end their marriage.

_____

7 Tess expected to suffer for murdering Alec d'Urberville.

_____

8 Angel and Tess looked for somewhere to stay for a few days.

_____

Published by Macmillan Heinemann ELT
Between Towns Road, Oxford OX4 3PP
Macmillan Heinemann ELT is an imprint of
Macmillan Publishers Limited
Companies and representatives throughout the world
Heinemann is a registered trademark of Harcourt Education, used under licence

ISBN 978 0 2300 3532 4
ISBN 978 1 4050 7457 5 (with CD pack)

This version of *Tess of the d'Urbervilles* by Thomas Hardy was retold by
John Escott for Macmillan Readers
First published 2005
Text © Macmillan Publishers Limited 2005
Design and illustration © Macmillan Publishers Limited 2005

This version first published 2005

Illustrated by Kay Dixey
Map on page 10 by Dave Burroughs
Cover by Getty Images \ The Gleaner by Joshua Cristall \ Bridgeman Art
Library.

Printed in Thailand
2010 2009 2008
5   4   3   2   1

with CD pack
2010 2009 2008
9   8   7   6   5